"Murder In Mind"
By
DEREK PETER ANSON

©2023

"All rights reserved."

Table of Contents

Chapter 1 1

Chapter 2 13

Chapter 3 21

Chapter 4 27

Chapter 5 34

Chapter 6 46

Chapter 7 53

Chapter 8 62

Chapter 9 69

Chapter 10 77

Chapter 11 88

Chapter 12 95

Chapter 13 107

Chapter 14 115

Chapter 15 121

Chapter 16 130

Chapter 17 142

Chapter 18 154

Chapter 19 161

Chapter 20 170

Chapter 21 180

Chapter 22.................................190

Chapter 23.................................205

Chapter 24.................................219

Chapter 25.................................225

Chapter 26.................................238

Chapter 27.................................243

Chapter 28.................................251

Chapter 29.................................265

Chapter 30.................................275

I Would like to dedicate this novel to my partner, he passed away last August of terminal cancer, he was my inspiration and he urged me to get this novel published.

Then I met my friend and writer/editor Steven Cohen and he made this realization happen, without his help and knowledge this would have never have been achieved.

Thank you to Steven, my family and friends for your continual support through this process.

CHAPTER ONE
Friday 16th December 2016, Stowgarth Town Centre.

At 4.15 pm.

The traffic around the one-way system that evening was bumper to bumper. The conditions outside were getting worse. The icy roads were dangerous and slippery. Detective Constable Kapoor was driving an unmarked Police car, Detective Sergeant Carruthers was riding shotgun. They were heading to the south of Stowgarth to the Halstead Council Estate, on a shout. There had been a robbery. It was nicknamed, 'Sodom and Gomorrah,' by the Police officers at the station.

The Off license was located on Edenfield Road; it was the main thoroughfare through the Halstead Council Estate. The area was renowned for petty crime and anti-social behavior, but the streets around the Council Estate were now paved with heroin and crack cocaine, drug dealing, and turf wars were the norm. The Off license was in a row of rundown brick shops, on the opposite side of the road was a brand-new building that looked out of place. It was the new community library and hub for local residents to meet-up. It had been funded by the Stowgarth Gazette Lottery. It had a very modern design.

It was built in a hexagonal shape. It had massive, long high glass windows. Its roof was tiled, and on one side it surprisingly had four solar panels positioned. Possibly generating enough electricity for the whole building.

There was a small, crowded gravel car park at the rear of the shops. DC Kapoor parallel parked the black top of the range 4x4 German car between a white van and a sparkling new Police car. DS Carruthers complimented him on an excellent manoeuvre, Carruthers own parking was much to be desired even though she had spent a year in the traffic division. She was going to cut her career short with the police force, but decided to apply to become a detective constable and pasted with flying colour's.

DS Carruthers was still getting used to working life in the Serious Crime Unit since her switch from Luton CID. The Serious Crime Unit was split into two teams, each team had a Detective Sergeant who oversaw them. DS Carruthers had been introduced to everyone in her team and she chose to work closely with DC Kapoor. She paired DC Dempster and DC Windass together.

DC Carruthers was fast approaching fifty, she was 5foot8 and she had a size 14 waist, her weight was always up and down. She was always on a faddy diet or something. She had jet black hair that was styled in a bob, and big watchful emerald eyes and a beauty spot on her right cheek. She spoke with a hoarse voice. Smoking was one of her many vices, like her weight she had tried to stop or cut down, but the slightest blip she was smoking heavily again.

    She put it down to the pressure of her job and she was sticking to that excuse. She was always a snappy dresser. She wore a black winter coat over a black trouser suit and a matching chunky woolen cardigan. DC Kapoor made sure the car was fully locked before they walked towards the Off license. He was a friendly guy with a dry sense of humor.

    He was an excellent Detective Constable. He was very well liked by his colleagues and the powers of be. He was a Detective Sergeant in the making. His family were from Chennai in Southern India, but he was born in Grantham, Lincolnshire. DC Kapoor was Sikh. He was in his late twenties, tall and he had a trim physique. He wore a black turban that hid his short cropped black hair. His fellow officers were envious of his well-kept full beard. He wore a grey parka over a stylish double breasted dark grey suit.

    The Off license was jam sandwiched between a betting shop and a chippy. The smell of fish, chips and vinegar permeated the air making the detectives feel very hungry. DC Kapoor noticed behind them was a group of youths in hoodies on mountain bikes gazing in their direction. DS Carruthers opened the door to the shop and went inside.

    The Off license was in disarray, things had been knocked over and the shelves behind the counter had been ransacked. A male uniformed officer was taking a statement from the owner of the shop. PC Sanders was 6foot4. His colleagues nicknamed him the 'Sugar Monster' because of the sheer size of him. He was in his early twenties; he was one of the youngest uniform officers at the station.

He had just successfully completed his probation period. Max was mixed race, he had wild hazel eyes, a shaved head and designer stubble.

DS Carruthers was at least 25 years older than him, but she still eyed him up and down and wondered what he would look like naked. DS Carruthers preferred younger men even though her estranged husband was much older than her. She thought that PC Sanders could be the one to satisfy her sexual needs, but she did not hold much hope.

PC Sanders pulled away from the shop owner and spoke to detectives,

"Are you the only uniformed officer?" DS Carruthers asked.

"Yes, most of us are patrolling alone, cutbacks and all that. Luckily, I was nearby in my squad car, so they requested me to come here. Someone else is bound to turn-up soon." PC Sanders smiled.

"There should be uniformed officers out there

seeing if anybody has seen anything." DC Kapoor scowled but he knew it was not the PC'S fault.

"What time did the robbery take place?" DS Carruthers asked.

"The armed robbers came in wielding baseball bats at about 3.40pm." PC Sanders answered.

"It's a funny time of the day, especially when the chippy next door is open and busy with customers."

"People around here do not care; they keep their mouths shut and do not come forward. Honor amongst thieves and all that." PC Sanders smiled.

"Can I speak to the owner?" DS Carruthers asked.

"This is Mr. Choudhry." PC Sanders introduced him. He was white as a sheet, and he was holding onto the counter with grim death.

Anwar Choudhry was in his late 60s. He was medium height and overweight.

He had greenish-blue sunken eyes, a thick mop of grey hair, unshaven and talked with a Pakistani accent. He wore a cream Salwar Kameez, a long knee shirt over loose fitting pants. On his head was a Taqiyah. It was a short-round cap made from a coarse cloth.

"I am Detective Sergeant Carruthers, and this is my colleague Detective Constable Kapoor."

They flashed their Police Warrant cards in his direction. A small lady appeared from the back of the shop.

"This is Maleeha, my wife." Mrs. Choudhry smiled. She looked older than her husband. She had shoulder length grey hair. She was wearing a traditional ladies blue and gold Salwar Kameez with a blue dupatta around her shoulders and it partly covered her head.

"Hello, are you the detectives?" She spoke softly and slowly. Her English was not as fluent as her husbands. The detectives introduced themselves again.

"Were you both here when the robbery took place?" DS Carruthers asked.

"Not just me, Maleeha was upstairs cooking dinner, my assistant takes over at 6pm. She works until 10pm then I come down and close-up."

"PC Sanders will carry on taking your statement, do you have CCTV cameras?"

"Yes." Mrs. Choudhry said.

"Can we see the footage of the robbery?"

"Yes, come this way." Mrs. Choudhry directed.

The detectives followed her into the backroom. On the way she pointed out the CCTV cameras dotted around the shop.

The back room was tiny and dark. The smell of cooking spices flavored the air. There was a small old-fashioned kitchenette with a yellow Formica table and two out of place carved wooden armchairs. There were cardboard boxes galore piled high to the ceiling. The detectives took a seat at the table.

"Are you and your husband from Pakistan?" DC Kapoor enquired.

"Yes, we grew up in Mughal Pura near Lahore. We married there in March 1968, and we moved over here in the seventies. We bought this shop from my elderly Uncle in 1986."

DS Carruthers sat disinterested; she was not one for chatting about trivial details. She just asked the relevant questions and did the job at hand. There was no room for frilly bits they just got in the way of business. There was an old chunky flatscreen television mounted to the wall. It was playing CCTV footage from the shop. Mrs.

Choudhry picked up the handset off the table and pointed it at the television. She rewound the footage to the robbery.

The detectives watched the fuzzy screen keenly. *They saw two men dressed in black jeans, black hoodies, black balaclavas, and black gloves entering the shop at 3.40pm wielding baseball bats. Mr. Choudhry was afraid, he did not put up a fight, he let them take what they wanted from the shop. There was a tall armed robber and a much smaller one. The tall armed robber made his way around to the till, he emptied the money into a black sports bag then he pushed Mr. Choudhry out of the way. Then he proceeded to empty the shelves of cigarettes and tobacco pouches.*

The tall armed robber found a box under the counter, again he tipped the contents in his bag. The smaller armed robber helped himself to things off the shelves, filled his bag with spirits and other expensive items. When they had ransacked the shop they made a quick getaway, leaving Mr. Choudhry devastated. The detectives looked at each other.

The armed robbery had the same M.O (Modus Operandi) as the other robbery that took place in Cheadley Heath, Stowgarth last weekend. They both knew the armed robber was getting confident and they were sure there would be more armed robberies to come. They needed to find or catch the culprits red handed before someone got hurt.

"Are you insured Mrs. Choudhry?" DS Carruthers asked.

"Yes, we are with the Victoria Insurance Company, Anwar will sort it out." Maleeha played with her dupatta around her shoulders.

"He was lucky he did not get hurt." DS Carruthers stated.

"Yes, let's be thankful for small mercies." DC Kapoor put together his hands in reverence.

DS Carruthers felt embarrassed. She had a catholic upbringing but never got her head around the religion; she only attended church for weddings, christenings, and funerals. Mrs. Choudhry was not Sikh, but she understood the universal religious significance. Maleeha handed her a copy of the CCTV footage. DS Carruthers thanked her and they made their way back into the shop.

DC Dempster and DC Windass had appeared at the crime scene. PC Sanders was standing at the counter making a long inventory of what had been taken from the shop. Maleeha went and stood by her husband.

"I am glad you are both here. DC Dempster can you ring SOCO and see where they are? They should be here by now."

"Yes, Serg." DC Dempster went to make the call outside.

"DC Windass can you and DC Dempster take over here, we are going back to the station." "Yes, Serg."

"DS Carruthers, I have spoken to control, and they are sending another uniform officer." PC Sanders interrupted.

"Good about time." DC Kapoor replied. "You shouldn't have to work on your own."

"Mr. Choudhry, before we go, can you remember the armed robbers' accents?" DS Carruthers interrupted abruptly.
"Like I said to that officer. They sounded local." Mr. Choudhry replied.

"Thank you, Mr. Choudhry, we will let you know how our investigation goes.

There are a lot of similarities with an armed robbery that took place in Cheadley Heath last weekend. We are trying our best to track these criminals down."

As the detectives left the shop, they bumped into DC Dempster who had just come off the phone with SOCO and they were on their way. The snow was falling heavier now. The group of teenagers in hoodies on mountain bikes had dispersed.

The unmarked Police car was under a thin covering of fresh snow. DC Kapoor started the engine and cleared the front and back window screens.

Suddenly there was a loud knock on the passenger's window. The detective's hearts missed a beat. An old man with a gnarled wooden walking stick steered at them. He was a strange looking man. He was as old as the hills and bald as a coot. He had a large bulbous nose and a long beard and black oversized spectacles. He was wearing an old scruffy grey overcoat and a blue woolen hat.

"Are you the Police?"

Yes, can I help you?" DS Carruthers asked.

"At about 3.45pm. I was coming for my fish supper. I had been in the library all afternoon and I was crossing Edenfield Road. I saw two armed robbers all in black with baseball bats and black sports bags run out of the Off license towards the car park. They got inside a green vehicle and drove off rapidly in the direction of Grayson. The registration number was 02 KLM."

Suddenly DS Carruthers phone rang, she asked the man to wait a moment while she took the call. It was the Chief.

A few minutes passed. She ended the call and spoke to the old man.

"Would you go over to the uniformed officer stood at the door and give him your statement please." She pointed to the uniformed officer.

DS Carruthers gained DC Windass attention who was stood talking to PC Sanders outside the off-license. DS Carruthers informed him that there had been a murder at the Stowgarth Catholic Church and they had to go.

CHAPTER TWO
Across town at the local Catholic Church.

DS Munro at Stowgarth Police Station was on annual leave and taking her daughter for her dance recital at St Augustine's Catholic Church. They were sitting having refreshments when an old friend of Kate's showed-up.

Sandra was a good friend but she married into money and she never stopped bragging about it. They continued chatting for around 20 minutes.

"How's your mum?" Sandra asked. She received a text message; upon checking it and her whole persona changed. She didn't give Kate time to answer her question. Sandra gave Kate and Gemma a quick kiss and hastily disappeared from the church hall.

"Are you ready to go home sweetheart?" Kate asked.

"Yes mummy, can we go and say goodbye to Mrs. Jefferson?"

They walked over to Gemma's dance teacher; she was standing in a group of women laughing. Kate recognized some of them as members of the church's Mothers Union, they raised needed funds for the church.

Mrs. Jefferson was a tall slim lady. She had short cropped blond curly hair and pale blue eyes. Mrs. Jefferson was flushed with pride; the dance recital had gone amazingly well. All their hard work had paid off.

Kate and Gemma wished her Merry Christmas and they walked towards the cloak room. Gemma put on her pink puffer jacket with a matching pink woolen scarf and gloves.

They went outside. It was dark and the stars twinkled high in the sky. The temperature had plummeted, and the snow was falling heavier than earlier. Kate spotted Sandra's red estate car still parked in the car park. Kate asked Gemma to stay on the church steps while she navigated the ice rink that had formed in the car park.

The red estate car was partly covered in ice and snow and the engine was running.

She walked carefully around to the driver's door. She did not want to slip on the icy ground. She noticed bloody footprints in the snow. She was careful not to tread on them. The driver's door was open.

"Sandra!!! Are you ok?" Kate shouted. There was no response.

Her detective training and experience came to the forefront of her mind. She avoided touching the car door. Kate peered inside the car. She put her hand over her mouth to stop herself from screaming and alarming Gemma.

Sandra and the car were bathed in blood; it looked like she had been the victim of a frenzied knife attack. Kate pulled away and threw up all over the frozen ground. She tried to compose herself, but she could not stop the tears rolling down her face. Kate checked to see if she was miraculously still breathing, but there was no sign of life. She fumbled for her phone from her coat pocket and rang the Stowgarth Police Station. The Serious Crime Unit and scene of crime officers were quickly dispatched to the scene.

Kate was rooted to the spot; she could not move a muscle. She tried to compose herself, but she was shaking terribly. Her best friend had been murdered right under her nose and she was not able to do anything about it. Kate reluctantly had to leave the crime scene, but she needed to make sure her daughter was safe.

The killer could have still been in the vicinity. Kate moved quickly but carefully not to disturb the crime scene. Gemma was still waiting alone frozen to the core on the Church steps. Kate took her by the hand, she looked back Sandra's car in dismay, her eyes welled up with tears again. She wiped her face with her black woolen glove and marched her daughter back inside the church.

Kate searched the church hall for Father Doyle. He was standing talking to the church verger next to the church hall's Christmas tree. It had been decorated beautifully by the local cub scout group. Father Doyle was a dotty old priest. He was small, round and bald. He had a plump deceptively sleepy face, an air of contentment, ambition achieved. Father Doyle wore small gold-colored rimmed spectacles. He wore a black cassock, a white knee cottar and around his neck was a gold stole.

Kate moved towards him.

"Father Doyle, sorry for interrupting but it's very important." Kate insisted. Father Doyle turned and smiled serenely.

"Calm down child, things cannot be that bad."

"They are Father Doyle." Kate's voice raced and she went white as a sheet. She explained what had happened outside in the car park, she didn't tell him who the victim was. Father Doyle was astounded by the disturbing news.

"I have phoned the Police. My colleagues are on their way. You need to make an announcement forbidding anyone to leave until the Police arrive."

Father Doyle walked gracefully into the Centre of the church hall gaining everyone's immediate attention. He stood with hands clasped with an apprehensive look on his face. He called for silence. He delivered the important news calmly and tactfully.

Everyone looked in disbelief, some of the old dears sobbed quietly in the background. Father Doyle reassured the people who had come to watch or take part in the dance recital that the Police were on the way and the car park was now a crime scene. He implored everyone to stay in the church hall until the police arrived. Kate saw the grim concerned faces on the parishioners. So, she jumped in to try and reassure them.

"I am a Detective Sergeant at Stowgarth

Police Station, DS Kate Munro, my colleagues will make sure the area around the church is safe, they will want to talk to you all individually…It be will best if we all separate and individually stand or sit alone until the officers come to take our statements….Also, because the carpark is now a crime scene. It will be up to the crime scene officers to choose which cars need to stay and which can go. If you are one of the unlucky ones, you will have to make arrangements to get home and return for your car tomorrow."

The church hall was big, so people there separated themselves without any problems.
Everyone looked more at ease, a lot of them were glad for the sanctuary of the church.

"Thank you, Kate." Father Doyle put his hands together in prayer. There was complete silence.

"Let us pray and ask God for guidance and protection through this horrible time."

DS Munro went to speak with the Church Verger. Who was a university dropout with long black hair and a shocking sense of fashion.

"Does the car park have CCTV?"

"Yes, it does. The best person to speak to is Charlie Whelan the Church Warden. He has just taken his mother back to her Nursing Home, but he will be back soon."

Kate walked over to the church doors. A fog was descending upon Stowgarth making the crime scene look even more eerie and sinister by the minute. The snow was still falling from the sky and there was a bitterly chilly wind blowing. The crime scene had been untouched. She thought about poor Sandra and wiped a tear from her cheek. She knew she could not go back to the crime scene, so she stood at the door watching the witnesses inside and the crime scene at the same time. DS Munro could hear sirens in the distance getting closer and closer.

A Police car arrived at the church carpark in dukes of Hazzard style with blue flashing lights. When it came to a stop it silenced its sirens. Two young male police constables alighted the vehicle. They saw Kate standing at the church doors and made their way over to her. Kate knew them from the station.

"Hiya boys."

"Hello, Kate." They said in unison.

She explained her findings, she told them that there were potential witnesses inside the church hall, and they were all staying there until they had given their statements.

"Thanks, Kate. We will cordon off the area and wait for your unit and SOCO to arrive." The older PC directed.

Kate stood at the church doors; she could not help but force a smile. The two uniformed officers were slipping and sliding all over the car park. They were trying to split the car park in two. The crime scene and potential witness's cars were cordoned off by police tape, the other half was going to be used by police vehicles.

CHAPTER THREE

Suddenly a shiny black Saloon car pulled into the car park. DCI Barnes got out the car and another detective followed behind him. They noticed Kate in the doorway to the church. They made their way over to her ignoring the police constables. DCI Barnes wore a dark grey trench coat and his hood was shielding him from the falling snow. It made him look taller and thinner than usual. The other man was DC Dimka. He was dark skinned, he wore a black sports winter coat, warm woolens on his hands, head around his neck.

"Hello, Kate, before we start do you know the victim?" DCI Barnes asked.

"Yes, it's my best friend Sandra de Villiers? She is a parishioner here."

"Sorry, to hear about your friend." DCI Barnes said with sympathy.

DC Dimka stood silently beside him.

"Can you tell me what you know?" DCI Barnes asked.

"I've been in the church for the past few hours, it was my daughters first dance recital this evening." Kate said proudly. She told them what happened, where and who was the victim.

"As you know Kate, I would love you on this case, but your personally involved." Thank you for looking after the crime scene and the potential witnesses in the church. You are a witness and you will have to make a statement." DCI Barnes said, irrevocably. Kate nodded and managed a smile. Her boss put his hand firmly on her shoulder, "We will find the person who did this." He reassured her.

"What is the victim's surname again?" DC Dimka asked.

"Her name is............." Kate took a second to compose herself. She did not want to cry in front of her fellow detectives.

"Her surname is de Villers and she lives with her husband, Johan de Villiers at the Old Granary in Trussington village." DC Dimka wrote the name and address on his notepad.

"Where you close friends?" DCI Barnes asked delicately, he could see she was very fragile at this moment.

"We went to Grammar School together, but we grew apart as we got older."

DCI Barnes reassured her, "Kate, if you had not found her and kept the crime scene free from contamination, we would not have the best chance of finding the killer."

"Does the car park have CCTV?" DC Dimka asked.

"Yes, the person to talk to is Charlie Whelan, but he left straight after the dance recital to take his mother home." Kate replied.

"The CCTV may have caught our culprit hanging around the car park…OR it could have caught the person hanging around the car park and who murdered our victim." DCI Barnes interjected.

A police traffic car arrived at the crime scene. DCI Barnes asked the two officers if they could set up a road block at the beginning and end of Church Street. He turned around and a dark blue mini bus with Lincolnshire Police Force emblazoned on it and two dog unit vans stopped just outside the car park on church street. It contained a team of uniformed officers. DCI Barnes marched over to them and briefed the highest ranked officer. The Sergeant was known for his efficiency. He barked his orders and sent his constables in various directions; some to take statements in the church, some to investigate the surrounding area, some to do a door to door on church street.

Then another vehicle pulled into the car park this time it had two detectives in it. As soon as they got out the car DCI Barnes brought them up to speed with everything.

"I'm the Senior Investigating Offer and DI Love will be my deputy. Larry's back tomorrow from four weeks in Honduras, so he will be ready for action." He laughed.

DCI Barnes explained what happened and to who, "DC Dimka is taking a statement from Kate in the church hall....DS Carruthers you and your team will assist.....Dog units are going to search the surrounding area, while uniformed officers do a door to door on Church Street. I am sure this fog will not help matters. SOCO are on their way... It could be a robbery that has gone terribly wrong, but that does not explain the text message she received before she was murdered. SheShe must have known her murderer. He or she must have lured the victim to her car then attacked her. We need to check the towns and church CCTV footage. We may see our killer. We need to make the appropriate searches and enquires...DS Carruthers, you and DC Kapor need to go give the bad news to her husband. DC Dimka has a copy of the address on his note pad...Are DC Dempster and DC Windass still at the robbery on the Halstead Estate?"

"They have just text me they are on the way here."

"That's good."

The freezing fog was getting thicker by the minute. A team of crime officers and an on-call Pathologist arrived at the crime scene. Dr Baker was the Pathologist. He was tall and rangy. He had shoulder length salt and pepper curly hair and a goatee beard. Dr Baker had been a Pathologist with the Lincolnshire Police for the last 35 years and was retiring in the new year.

Dr Baker and his team of crime scene investigators donned their lightweight white overalls, masks, gloves and overshoes before entering the crime scene. SOCO erected a tent over the car. Dr Baker instructed his team to collect, preserve and catalogue as much evidence as possible.

A young female scene of crime officer photographed the body while four others took various samples from the car and the surrounding area. An older man with slug brown eyebrows that merged in the middle had possibly found the murder weapon. It had lay undiscovered in the snow about 100 yards from the car. He had also found bloody footprints in the snow heading in the direction of Church Street. He told the Pathologist his findings.

Dr Baker took a look at the possible murder weapon. The crime scene officer handed him a polythene bag, "I photographed it in situ, carefully bagged it and catalogued it." The dagger was covered in blood. It was an antique, it had an ivory handle and a strong blade. It was 20cms in length and it weighed around 190 grams. The scene of the crime scene officer assumed it was the only murder weapon, but Dr Baker said, "Things aren't always what they seem, you know that by now…..I'm nearly done here and I need to go and see the SIO. Can you make arrangements for the body to be removed and taken to the mortuary."

CHAPTER FOUR

DC Dempster and DC Windass had not long arrived when they are asked by the DCI if they could find out if Charlie Whelan the church warden had returned, he needed questioning immediately and they urgently needed to see the CCTV footage of the car park.

"What time was the murder?" DC Dempster asked.

"Sandra left the church hall around 5.00pm and Kate found her murdered in her car about 10 minutes later." DCI Barnes replied.

The church hall was a hive of activity, a lot of people had given their statements and were now waiting to see if they could go home in their cars. But it was very unlikely that SOCO were going to let cars in the car park leave while were still investigating the crime scene.

The detectives went over to a young police constable, she was standing next to a table that had canisters of hot tea, coffee and soup. The beverages table was always a big hit at these events. DC Windass collected two cups of tea. The drinks were free for the people who had to stay behind, but he gave her two shiny two-pound coins. The old lady who dispensed the tea, was very thankful and put it in her money pot.

"All proceeds go to the church." She remarked. DC Windass smiled and handed DC Dempster his cup of tea.

DC Dempster spotted a female officer speaking to elderly woman. He marched over to her with purpose. The police constable was medium height and weight. She had short auburn hair and pale blue eyes.

"Hiya DC Dempster."

"Hiya." They both smiled, there was an awkward silence.

"Do you know which man is Charlie Whelan the church warden?" DC Dempster asked.

"He's over there." She pointed to an old man who was sat eating a sandwich on the stairs to the stage. The church warden was nearly bald. He was tall and grossly overweight. He had national health glasses over brown sunken eyes. He wore dirty khaki trousers, brown boots and a dark blue ribbed oversized woollen jumper. The detectives walked over to him.

"You've shagged her, haven't you?" DC Windass laughed. DC Dempster smiled.

"Only once, we were both drunk." DC Dempster laughed. DC Windass grinned.

"Are you Mr Whelan?" DC Dempster asked.

"Yes, I am who's asking?" Mr Whelan was annoyed by the interruption.

"I am Detective Constable Dempster and this is my colleague Detective Constable Windass. I need to ask some questions and DC Windass will be taking notes."

"Sorry, I am just worried about my mother, she didn't seem herself today. How can I help you?" Mr Whelan forced a smile.

"As you may know, someone was murdered out in the car park." DC Dempster said.

"Is it true that Sandra de Villiers was the victim?"

"Hard to say at this point, we need a formal identification…Can we look at the CCTV footage for the car park?"

"Sorry, the cameras were vandalised and we don't have the funds available to replace them." Mr Whelan apologised.

"That's a shame. When did you last see Sandra de Villiers?" DC Dempster probed.

"I sat with her at the back of the church. She came in five or ten minutes late."

"Did you know Mrs de Villiers well?"

"Yes, of course, she comes to early morning mass on a Monday and Wednesday. To be honest I know her husband better because he is my dentist."

"I understand you took your mother home. What time was that?"

"We left straight after the dance recital finished. I think it was about 4.50 pm. My mum lives in the Ravensdale Nursing Home in Grayson. I got back here about ten minutes ago. I wanted to speak to my girlfriend, but I was told that you needed to speak to me first."

"Did you see anybody looking shifty in the car park when you left for the nursing home?"

"No, I don't think so." He paused and continued. "Wait a minute! There was a man slipping and sliding along church street. He was going in the direction of Gorton Road."

"Are you sure it was a man?" DC Dempster probed further.

"Yes, I saw him in my car headlights as I turned onto Church Street."

"What was he wearing?"

"He wore a dark green wax jacket. He had a canary yellow and green woolly hat and scarf on."

"Could you tell how old he was?"

"Not really."

"Anything else you can to tell us?"

"No that's all."

"Thanks Mr Whelan you have been very informative."

DC Dempster looked at his fellow detective then left the building.

DCI Barnes was on his mobile phone when DC Dempster made an appearance by his side.

"Thanks SIR." He then ended the call. "Sorry about that DC Dempster it was the Chief Super. Did you manage to speak to the church warden?" DC

Dempster told him his findings.

"Do you think he is a possible suspect?" DC Dempster asked.

"He knew the CCTV was not working, he left around 4.50pm, but that does not mean he did not wait around to kill our victim. He says he saw a man slipping and sliding along church street again it could be just fabrication." DCI Barnes assumed. "He has an alibi, but we will look into it."

DC Windass came out of the church. He slipped on the last step and fell on his bottom. He got up quickly, red faced, patting the snow off his parka. The DCI and DC Dempster just grinned at each other, but said nothing.

"DC Windass, did you get Charlie Whelan's car registration?" DCI Barnes asked.

"Yes. He drives a clapped-out silver vehicle. The Registration number is............" He flicked through his notepad. "96 JTT."

"Thanks. Now you are both here, I have some up-to-date news. The dog unit found some bloody footprints on church street they headed towards Gorton Road. He either jumped in a parked car or somebody was waiting for him. Uniformed are doing a door to door on Gorton Road."

"So, he might have an accomplice?" DC Dempster asked.

"It's a possibility."

"Were there any tyre tread marks to work on?" DC Windass asked.

"Too many, it's a very busy road." DCI Barnes sighed. "Can you collate the statements so we can all go over them tomorrow. See if there are inconsistencies or possible leads. Me and DC Dimka are waiting for SOCO to finish so we can have a look at the crime scene. DS Carruthers and DC Kapoor have gone to give the bad news to the victim's husband Johan de Villiers."

CHAPTER FIVE
Friday 16th December 2016, 7.00pm

DC Kapoor was an exceptionally good driver, but the conditions were dangerous. The fog was thicker out of the town centre. The village of Trussington was on the outskirts of Stowgarth. The quickest way to get there was by taking the A2580 to St Enoch's and getting off at junction 5. The A2580 was heavily congested with vehicles all traveling a lot slower than normal speed. The journey took 20 minutes longer than expected.

Trussington was a little village, it was like a scene from a Christmas card. All the gardens and roofs of the houses had a glistening blanket of snow. Most of them were illuminated with Christmas lights while others were in darkness. The occupants were either out or tucked up in bed. Thankfully the pavements and roads had all been gritted. The old granary was easy to find. It was located on Kiln Lane next to the old village hall. It was a two-storey stone building with lots of character and tastefully decorated in Christmas lights. There was a new top of the range 2016 German black sports car in the driveway. They assumed it was owned by Johan de Villiers. DS Carruthers wrote down its registration on her note pad ST16 JDV. As they parked behind it, a security light came on blinding them. They got out of the unmarked police car. The driveway, garden and pathway were under a white covering of undiscovered snow. It was very slippery under foot. As they approached the porch light came on and a man appeared in the doorway. He was tall and thickset. He wore grey jogging bottoms, his muscles bulged out of his black sweater. He had a fair complexion, deep blue eyes and blond slicked back hair. Johan de Villiers looked like a nightclub bouncer not a dentist.

"I heard you pull up in the driveway, I thought you were my wife. It's late can I help?" Johan asked in a South African accent. The detectives showed him their police warrants.

"Is Sandra, OK?"

"Can we come in Mr de Villers?" DS Carruthers.

The smell of fresh paint overwhelmed them as they entered the hallway. The walls had been painted in a pastel green colour. The floor was covered in plastic sheeting, it rippled under their feet. Pots and trays of paint were dotted around, and the woodwork and radiator were unfinished. A sparkling chandelier hung high in the ceiling. She had not seen one like that since she visited Chatsworth house in Derbyshire one Christmas with her nan and grandad. The chandelier was a lot smaller, but it was just as magnificent. There was a black wrought iron spiral staircase that ascended upwards to the floor above. The detectives were shown into a light, airy rectangular shaped lounge. The room had also just been decorated, the walls were magnolia. A beautiful real Christmas tree was standing in the corner next to the wooden Welsh dresser. It was heavily decorated in all different coloured lights and baubles of every shape and colour. Underneath was a traditional nativity scene. The figurines were about 12inchs high and made out of Italian resin. You could see they were expensive. They had been positioned carefully; you could see that the person who had worked on this scene had a very creative flair.

There was a large burnt orange round shaped shaggy carpet on the light wooden parquet flooring. The long pencil curtains in the windows and the cushions on the sofa and chairs were rich warm autumn colours (golden browns, ruby reds, pumpkin, and spicy nutmeg). The furniture was modern in taste. There was a blazing coal fire in the centre of the room; it had a light oak fire surround. There was a 75inch black Samsung flatscreen television mounted on the wall.

It looked brand new just out of its box. Faith glanced at her mobile phone; it was 7.40 pm. She knew she was not going to get home until around midnight then she was back at work at 8am.

Johan asked them to take a seat. They sat down on a brown leather sofa. It instantly sucked them in. Faith thought *I'm so tired, I could just kick off my shoes and curl up and go to sleep.* Faith admired the three beautiful large autumn landscape paintings on the wall and wondered if they been painted by Johan or his wife. Faith loved ART. She went to Art College after leaving secondary school she was very good at it, but her heart was not in it. She wanted to join the police force so she could become a detective like her dad.

Suddenly from nowhere they were pounced on by two extremely energetic and playful Golden Retrievers. They fought for the visitor's attention. Johan quickly apologised and ushered them back into the kitchen.

"Sorry they got through the dog gate." Johan laughed. "Now, may ask about my wife?"

"You'd better take a seat." DS Carruthers insisted. Johan took a seat in a wooden rocking chair opposite them.

"That does not sound good has there been an accident?"

"I am sorry to tell you that at about 5pm tonight your wife was attacked and killed in her car in the Catholic Church car park in Stowgarth." DS

Carruthers voice was slow careful and sincere. Johan put a hand to his mouth in shock.

"How? Why? Not Sandra."

"Sandra was seen at the Catholic Church dance recital. One of our off-duty colleagues, spoke to her in the church hall. Sandra received a text and quickly disappeared. My colleague and her daughter went out to the car park to get in her car when she saw Sandra's car was still there. She went to see she was ok and found that she had been attacked and she was not breathing. Forensics are now at the crime scene, hopefully they will find some evidence to identify the suspect."

"Do you want us to call someone to sit with you?" DC Kapoor asked.

"No, I will be fine. I deal with things better on my own."

"Our colleague said that Sandra had a red leather bag and a mobile phone. Before I left, I asked if SOCO had found it, but it was not at the crime scene." DS Carruthers added.

"Was it a robbery?" Johan interrupted. DS Carruthers thought: *He was hoping for a possible explanation or was he deflecting the suspicion off himself.*

"We are not sure?" DS Carruthers said. There was an uneasy silence.

"When did you last see your wife?"

"She came home around 3.30pm from a dog show. She dropped off Norma and Cassidy and went out to the dance recital at the Catholic church."

"Do you know of anybody who may have wanted to hurt her?" DS Carruthers spoke slower, the delicate question hung in the air. Johan was surprised by her bluntness.

"Everyone loved Sandra. She was great to be around, she had an infectious laugh, and she didn't take fools gladly."

"Is there anybody you want us to contact for you?"

"Sandra's parents live in Vancouver in Canada; it will be best if I speak to them."

"OK...Do you know what type of mobile phone Sandra had?"

"She had a brand-new mobile like mine. Both our phones are on contract."

"Do you have an update copy of her mobile

phone bill?"

"Not at hand, I will have to go up to my office and get one." Johan looked perplexed.

"Can we have a copy of yours as well Mr de Villiers?"

He wasn't impressed, but he scuttled upstairs with his tail firmly between his legs. Faith got up from the sofa and went to look through the patio doors at the end of the lounge. By surprise there was a large conservatory attached to the property. It was in total darkness. She flicked the light switch on. The conservatory was instantly bathed in bright light. The burnt orange roman blinds had been pulled down. The floor was tiled, it was designed like a chessboard. There were two Lloyd Loom wicker chairs and an extremely looking red chaise longue. There was a large burnt orange oval shaggy rug and a chrome and glass workstation stood in the middle. There was an out of place wooden tall bookcase, it was full of hard and paperback books. Johan came downstairs and appeared back in the lounge clutching some paperwork.

"Do you like the conservatory?" Johan asked.

"Yes, it's nice." DS Carruthers took a seat back on the sofa.

"We had it built when we first moved in. It was Sandra's space, she loved reading and writing in there." He handed her the relevant information.

"Johan, sit down, we need to ask you some more questions?" DS Carruthers sat forward in her seat. "I have to ask you, where were you between 4pm and 6pm."

"I have been here all day, I didn't go into work, I worked from home." Johan replied. "Hold on a minute, you don't think I killed my wife." He stood up furious. DC Kapoor raised his voice and asked him to sit and calm down.

"Can anyone verify your alibi?"

"Mrs Sweeting my housekeeper was here from 9am until midday then she came back to finish the ironing that was around 2pm. She stayed until 4.00pm then I was on my own all evening until you both came."

"So, nobody can actually verify your alibi? Between the hours of 4 and 7pm." DS Carruthers went straight for the throat.

"I WAS HERE ON MY OWN." Johan boomed.

"OK, you said you saw Sandra at 3.30pm.

Where had she been?" DS Carruthers looked at DC Kapoor and he continued the questioning.

"Like I said she was at a dog show." Johan snapped.

"Where?"

"She had been at a Championship Dog show at the Peterborough Showground in Cambridgeshire."

"How was she when she arrived home?"

"She was in a good mood because she had won a first in her first adult class with Norma, but she was in a rush because she was late for the dance recital."

"What has she been like the weeks coming up to today?"

"Alright, I do not know if this helps, but Sandra had her car damaged twice at dog shows. Sandra assumed it was because she had won again with Norma and Cassidy in the Puppy classes. Dog showing is a very jealous world and very fickle. Sandra just took no notice and shrugged it off."

"Have there been any other incidents?"

"No. Not what I am aware of. I do not know why, but she has been very secretive of late."

"Do you think she was having an affair?"

"It crossed my mind yes; it would explain a few things." Johan pulled a strange face and fidgeted in his rocking chair, "She received calls on her mobile phone and walked into the conservatory to talk. She received random texts messages at strange hours of the day. She was spending more money than usual. When she went out, she would return late and make lame excuses. I knew she was hiding something." Johan continued.

"Did Sandra have any money worries?" Johan nearly fell off his rocking chair laughing.

"No, we have enough money. Sandra did not have to work, she did not have to do the cooking, cleaning or ironing. All she did everyday was pamper herself at the local beauty parlour, go to the gym and dance studio. She groomed, bred golden retrievers and entered them into nationwide dog shows. Dog showing was her passion and she excelled at it. She taught ballroom and Latin dancing to children and adults on a Wednesday and Thursday evening at the Molinari school of dance in Grayson. If she did have any worries, I do not know what about?" Johan grinned sardonically. DS Carruthers wasn't completely satisfied with this so-called loving husband charade.

"Can we have your housekeepers name and address? We will need to question her?"

"I do not think she will be able to help you?"

"WE WILL BE THE JUDGE OF THAT MR DE VILLERS." DS Carruthers interrupted sharply.

"Mrs Sweeting lives at 5 Tennyson Close, here in Trussington. Her contact number is 070059832255." Johan sighed.

"Thank you, Johan." DS Carruthers said calm and polite. DC Kapoor scribbled it down in his note pad. DS Carruthers looked at her partner and they ended the questioning. There was a loud knock at the front door.

"That will be a Police Constable. He or she will keep an eye on you and what you do until SOCO arrive, then they will search the property."
"WHAT FOR! THAT CAN NOT BE RIGHT!" Johan boomed.

"Calm down Mr de Villiers, it's to gain as much as we can about Sandra and her life, any information gained will help the investigation." DS Carruthers replied.

Johan just mumbled.

"We will also need you to come and officially identify Sandra's body. We will call you after the Pathologist has done the post-mortem in the morning."

The detectives got up from the sofa, leaving their imprints behind. Johan stood up quickly and directed them towards the hallway. Johan opened the front door. DS Carruthers was pleased to see PC Sanders standing there. DS Carruthers handed Johan a card with the Serious Crime Units contact telephone number on it.
"We are sorry for your loss. We will keep you informed how the investigation goes."
Johan gritted his teeth and said thank you. DS Carruthers eyed and smiled at PC Sanders, and they walked back to the unmarked police car.

CHAPTER SIX

All you could hear was the snow crunching under the detective's feet. The night air was bitterly cold; it chilled them to the bone. Faith wearily gazed at her mobile phone it was 8.30pm. The car was under a thin layer of snow. DC Kapoor had to clear the windscreen, but they were soon on their way back up the A2580 towards Stowgarth. The detectives had plenty to mull over.

"What do you think about Mr de Villiers not having an alibi at the time of the murder?" DC Kapoor began.

"Well, he had enough time to drive to Stowgarth, park up on Gorton Road, murder his wife, and return home. That probably explains the text she received before she left the church. Did you notice when I asked him several questions that he answered quickly, with one-word answers and swiftly moved on changing the subject. Then he wouldn't give us the telephone number for the Molinari School of Dance. I think he was just pissed with us being there." DS Carruthers smiled.

"He will not be happy when SOCO turn up and take his house apart." DC Kapoor returned the smile.

"He seemed in a hurry to see us go. The

forensics and the town's CCTV footage will help us find out if he killed his wife. If we are wrong, he is definitely hiding something."

"What did you think about Mr de Villiers assumption about his wife having an affair?" DC Kapoor asked.

"Possible, I wouldn't want to be with a creep like that."

"A possible motive for murder." DC Kapoor pointed out.

"Exactly, watch this space, if there are no forensics, we will have to wait for him to slip-up and we will be there to catch him." DS Carruthers laughed.

DS Carruthers rang DCI Barnes and briefed him with what was said at Mr de Villiers home. He was pleased with their findings. He said that the other detectives had gone back to the station and could he be picked up from the crime scene.

When they arrived back to the crime scene it had started snowing again. It was still a hive of activity; uniformed police officers were still patrolling the crime scene and surrounding area. Church Street and now Gorton Road was blocked off to traffic, and the public who didn't live there.

SOCO were still gathering evidence, but the victim had been removed and taken to the Mortuary. DCI Barnes stood waiting for their appearance, he was talking to the priest at the doorway to the church, he waved in their direction. 5 minutes later he joined them both in the car. DC Kapoor sped off in the desired direction. Stowgarth Police Station was built in the early 90s. It was made of brick with oversized UPVC tinted bullet proof windows. It had hard dark blue vertical corrugated metal cladding. STOWGARTH POLICE STATION was emblazoned in black lettering across the front of the building. It was illuminated tonight. It had four floors and a tiled roof. The Police station was having a complete overall. It was being re-modernized and re-furbished. The basement and ground floor had gone through major developments. At the time it caused chaos, but the departments were now reaping the benefits. The basement had a new pathology suite (mortuary), forensic and ballistics laboratories. On the ground floor was the custody suite, it had a new custody desk and booking-in system. The cells were bigger, and the interview rooms were all covered by CCTV. The interview rooms had adjacent observation rooms for monitoring and training. The reception for the general public was light and airy and comfortable to wait in. Police control was totally upgraded. The remaining floors were in the proceeds of being cosmetically decorated, new furniture and technical equipment were going to replace the old and archaic. The first floor was for uniformed personnel and the staff canteen. The second floor was the Serious Crime Unit. The third floor was for top brass, human resources and administration. The top floor was home to the drug and vice squad. The police station had about 1000 operational police staff.

The Serious Crime Unit was as chaotic as ever. A new murder case had brought a fresh breath of air throughout the unit and the whole team wanted to be part of it.

DCI Barnes briefed the whole unit. The DCI was suave and sophisticated. In his fifties, short grey spiky hair and a well-groomed beard, deep set brown eyes and a cute smile. He was wearing a three-piece black pinstripe suit, white shirt and a red tie.

The briefing didn't take long, they had all been on since 8am that morning. DCI Barnes announced the team working on the murder case; I'm the SHO, DI Love will be my Deputy he is back on tomorrow's shift. Detective Sergeant Carruthers and Detective Constable Kapoor, Dempster, Windass and Dimka will also so be on the investigation...We have a problem, there was another armed robbery this evening. It was at the Edenfield Road off-licence on the Halstead Estate. They are gaining confidence, but I'm worried a member of the public are going to get hurt…DS Munro will be leading that investigation. Her team will be DC Brooks, DC Clarke and DC Edwards…I've just come off the phone with the Chief Super, he wants us all on our 'A' game. He wants diligence and efficiency, and he wants these two cases solved before he retires at the end of the year…I'm staying here with DC Dimka for the next couple of hours. The rest of you can go home, don't sleep too deep because you are all on call. If anything, materialisers you will be the first to know about it and I want you all here early because it's going to be a very busy day.

DS Carruthers car had been written off, she unluckily was hit by an uninsured driver and careered into some stationary vehicles. DC Kapoor picked her up every day and drove her to and from the police station.

"Shall we grab something to eat in the canteen, it's getting late now, and I'm fed up with pizzas or shish kebabs. It's my treat." DS Carruthers smiled.

The canteen was a ghost town this evening. The two detectives were the only one's dining. A pretty young girl was wiping down the tables and they could hear canteen staff clanging pots and pans in the kitchen. Detective Carruthers chose a table in front of the main windows that looked onto the floodlit staff car park. They took a seat facing each other. They tucked into their food. DS Carruthers had steak and kidney steam pudding, mushy peas, new potatoes and smothered with gravy. DC Kapoor had a vegetable risotto.

Suddenly her mobile phone rang, DS Carruthers had an idea who it would be. She retrieved it from her coat pocket that was resting on the back of her chair.

"Hello." DS Carruthers said. There was just heavy breathing, "Fuck Off Nob head." She said abruptly and ended the call.

"Who was that?" DC Kapoor enquired.

"Somebody is playing bloody games. I have been having these calls all week. I have had two calls today."

"Is it from a mobile number?"

"Yes, it's always the same number, when I ring it back it just keeps ringing."

"Block it then." DC Kapoor in a demanding tone.
"I don't know how too?" DS Carruthers replied, her cheeks went blood red. "I can only just operate my office laptop."

"Give it here and I will block it?" DS Carruthers handed him her phone. DC Kapoor tapped a few buttons and handed it back.

"Thanks." DS Carruthers smiled.

"By the way, what was the tune on your mobile phone?"

"Faith by George Michael."

"Cool." DC Kapoor did not want to look stupid, but he had never heard of it.

"Thanks for chauffeuring me about, I should get my car back in the new year." DS Carruthers reached over the table and touched his hand, "Thank you."

"That's fine, I don't mind." DC Kapoor smiled. "Anyway, I think I better get you home soon as you have eaten. Tomorrow is going to be a very busy day.

"Yes, I suppose."

CHAPTER SEVEN
Saturday 17th December 2016
The Serious Crime Unit 8am.

DCI Barnes Harry Barnes briefed his selected murder team. When his deputy DI Love appeared by his side everyone clapped and jeered. DI Love was a well-liked member of the Serious Crime Unit. He was in his middle sixties, and he was retiring on Christmas Eve. He had been a detective for 35 years. He stood 6foot2 and pissy thin, with a bald head, clean shaven and had hazel eyes under rimless glasses.

DCI Barnes pointed to the victims photograph on the evidence board.

"38-year-old Sandra de Villiers was the victim of a frenzied knife attack. She was found dead in her car in the car park of Stowgarth Catholic Church by one of our colleagues DS Munro. DS Munro was there to watch her daughters first dance recital. When she bumped into her best friend from grammar school, our victim Sandra de Villiers. Our victim was in a brilliant mood until she received a text message, her whole persona changed and she left the church hall at 5pm. DS Munro then found her murdered ten minutes later." DCI Barnes pointed to the photograph of the blood-stained antique dagger on the evidence board. "The murder weapon was found at the crime scene and is now with forensics. We are assuming there is only one killer, bloody footprints were found in the snow at the scene and they headed in the direction of Gorton Road. The bloody footprints stopped dead at the end of the road. We assume the killer got into a vehicle and disappeared. Uniformed did a door-to-door last night, but nobody saw the suspect or unknown vehicle. DS Munro said Sandra had a red leather handbag and an iPhone, but they were not found at the crime scene. SOCO have taken the relevant forensics and Dr Baker is doing the post-mortem this morning. We should have some results later today. The CCTV cameras in the church hall car park and have been out of action a while. DC Matthews, can you get onto Stowgarth Town Council and get them to send all1 the CCTV footage from the surrounding area over to us."

"What's the timeline, Guv?" DC Matthews piped-up.

"Sandra drove from Trussington Village to the Stowgarth Catholic Church. So, we should be looking at 4pm until 7pm. Can you and Alice do an ANPR check on her brand-new red estate the registration is S16 SDV. Her husband Johan de Villiers does not have an alibi for the hours between 4 pm and 7.40pm Yesterday evening. Can you do an ANPR check to see if his black sports car was seen in Stowgarth at the time of the murder. The registration is S16 JDV. A man was seen slipping and sliding along Church Street approximately 4.50pm. He is wearing a dark green wax jacket and green and canary yellow woolly hat and scarf. You should see him entering Church Street and you may see which direction he came from? Look for somebody coming out of Church Street after 5.10pm. Do they look shifty, you might even see somebody dump the victim's handbag. That's for you and DC Booth to be getting on with." The detectives went to their section at the back of the incident room.

"Our other suspect is Mr Whelan on all accounts he is an unusual individual. He sat with Sandra de Villiers at the back of the church hall. According to Mr Whelan the victim was ten minutes late to the dance recital. We need to check his alibi that he was in fact driving his mother back to the nursing home in Grayson at the time of the murder. Was the man slipping and sliding along Church Street real or fabrication we will find out?" He paused then shouted at the top of his voice. "DC Windass, SORRY IF THIS IS BORING YOU." DC Windass jumped out of his skin and rolled across the floor. "Yes, guv." He had not woken up properly, he had another sleepless night. His daughter 'Emily' was only 4 weeks old. His girlfriend 'Maria' was exhausted, she had been looking after him all day every day. They decided to change to bottle feeding so DC Windass could take on the night feeds. To be honest after three nights of hardly any sleep, he was starting to regret the decision.

"Please stay awake!!! DC Dimka went over Sandra's and Johan's mobile phone bills earlier this morning, they were for the month of November. So, he emailed the provider for an up-to-date record. DC Dimka is on duty at 12 midday, as he worked into the early hours with me…Uniformed took many statements from the church hall last night. They are all saying the same thing, they remember the victim leaving or they didn't see her at all. SOCO was so busy last night that the day shift is now investigating the victims home address. So that's what we know so far and what we need to do? DC Dimka is going to go through the criminal records of our suspects and other people that were present at the Dance Recital…Thank you folks, we all have plenty to get on with." DCI Barnes ended the briefing and walked towards his office, he turned back around and beckoned DS Carruthers to join him and DI Love.

"Yes, guv?" DS Carruthers appeared in the doorway.

"Come and sit down." The DCI directed, "I have DC Kapoor's statement from Mr Whelan the church warden. Can you and DC Kapoor go and follow it up?"

"Yes, guv."

"We will get the results of the blood samples tomorrow morning, but as you know DNA samples will take up to two weeks, but I'm sure with Detective Chief Superintendent Hargreaves influence we may get them quicker as he wants this solved before he retires."

DS Carruthers and the DCI were talking about the investigation when they were interrupted by DCS Hargreaves. DCI Barnes dismissed her; she closed the door behind her and went to give her team their orders.

"Serg." DC Kapoor put a hand on her shoulder. "The town's CCTV does not cover Edenfield Road. It only covers the high street, the market place and the one-way system around the town centre. I've rang the Ravensdale Nursing home for assistance. I have spoken to the home's secretary. There are some members of the staff that were on yesterday's afternoon shift. They finish at 2pm. So, I said we would be going over to take statements.

"Good work." DS Carruthers praised him.

The Nursing home car park was nearly full. DC Kapoor managed to park the unmarked police car next to a clapped green fluorescent three-wheeler. They got out the car, the wind was bitterly cold and the ground was slushy under foot. The Nursing home was purpose built, it looked like a fortress from the outside, all it was missing was bars at the windows and barb wired fencing.

The entrance was a series of glass doors probably designed to confuse residents if they decided to make a run for it. The reception was warm and welcoming, the smell of stale urine was recognisable over a cloud of well-intentioned floral air freshener. A large round woman with dashing white curly hair appeared from an office.

"Hello, I'm the nursing home manager."

The detectives flashed their police warrants in her direction and introduced themselves.

"I understand Mrs Whelan is a resident here?" DS Carruthers asked.

"Yes, she is our longest resident. She's been here longer than I have." The nursing home manager laughed.

"All we are doing is checking what time Mr Whelan brought his mother home."

"Yes ok, you spoke to our secretary. We have some carers on shift today that will be able to help you."

"Mrs Parson's, do you have CCTV in the building?" DC Kapoor enquired.

"The owners keep on saying it's going to be installed, but nothing has come of it yet." She laughed again. She then arranged for the carers to be interviewed in the dining room.

The dining room in the Nursing home was bright and ventilated. The carers seemed friendly enough. They were a funny looking bunch of individuals, all young, immature and you could see there was not a brain cell between them. The carers were dressed in purple uniforms. The detectives interrogated them individually. They were all female except for one young lad he had more mince than Dewhurst. The process took about 20 minutes. The last carer was Meg Manners, she was interviewed by DC Kapoor. Meg was in her late teens, she was thin as a rake, she had shocking pink shoulder length hair and smelled like an ashtray.

"Do you know what time Mr Whelan brought back his mother from the Stowgarth Catholic Church?"

"Yes, he brought Josephine home later than expected, it was around 5.50pm. I had just come off my break. He was in a foul mood. Usually, he undresses his mother and puts her to bed, but he just wheeled her into the lounge and stormed back out to his car."

"What kind of person is Mr Whelan?" DC Kapoor asked.

"Well, he's devoted to his mother, he comes every day to see her."

"Is he liked by you and your fellow carers?"

"To be honest he gives us carers the creeps."

"Why?" DC Kapoor probed further.

"He is a mummy's boy, he laughs and says pervy jokes, he's a grubby old man."

"Why do say he's grubby?"

"Have you met his girlfriend, she is two years older than me, she went to secondary school with my sister. She said she was weird too."

"Why?"

"Well, Mr Whelan is thirty years older than her, he's old enough to be her grandad. Have you met him? he's not the type of man you would take home to your mother and father." Meg giggled like a school girl. DC Kapoor took her statement and thanked her for her help. The detectives thanked the staff and went out to the car.

On the way back to the Police station the detectives talked through the statements. It was very clear that Mr Whelan was not liked by the carers. And they all said he arrived late at the nursing home about 5.50pm.

"His alibi is now up for scrutiny. It wouldn't have taken him an hour to get to the Ravensdale Nursing home from the Catholic Church. So where had he been? Did he wait for his victim to come out to her car? Was he the mystery caller?" DS Carruthers concluded, "I think we need to bring him in Mr Whelan for further questioning."

The detectives arrived back at the police station. DCI Barnes had gone to the canteen for a late breakfast. DS Carruthers relayed their findings to DI Love. He was counting down the days to his impending retirement. He had brought and was refurbishing an old narrow boat that he was planning to live on eventually on the Norfolk broads. DI Love was pleased with the developments and he said he would tell the DCI when he came back to the incident room. DS Carruthers went to find DC Dempster and DC Windass, they were at their desks. DS Carruthers asked them to go and bring Mr Whelan in for further questioning.

CHAPTER EIGHT

It was just after 1pm, snowflakes had started to fall from the sky over Stowgarth. The Police Station car park was virtually full of squad cars marked and unmarked. DC Dempster parked next to the DCI's black jaguar XE. DC Windass escorted Mr Whelan through to reception while DC Dempster went to find DS Carruthers.

"Where have all these people come from?" DC Windass laughed.

The reception seating was like a swarm of bees around a honey pot. The queen bee was a thickset girl in her twenties with long bleached hair and large pendulous breasts that had come along with a noisy brood of infants all under the age of six. They were causing havoc in the seating area to the disgruntlement of the people waiting.

"Take a seat Mr Whelan." DC Dempster directed. "I will let reception know that you are waiting for your solicitor."

Mr Whelan sat down in an empty seat, his demeanour had changed, he looked like the condemned man waiting for his fate to be sealed.

DCI Barnes the Senior Investigating Officer and DS Carruthers entered the room. DI Love and

DC Kapoor watched from the observational room next door. Mr Whelan looked very uncomfortable. He had sweat on his forehead and he slouched in his chair. Next to him sat his Solicitor. Mr Wade was from Wade and Shearing's solicitors in the Market place. He was a funny looking man, short and heavy. He was in his late fifties. Mr Whelan was wearing dirty brown corduroy trousers and a grey knitted jumper. DS Carruthers pressed the record button on the digital recorder. Everyone around the tables introduced themselves in turn.

DS Carruthers stated the date and time. She asked some basic questions then handed the questioning over to DCI Barnes.

"We have looked over the statements from the carers at Ravensdale Nursing home and it becomes evident that you did take your mother back home, but it appears that you didn't get there until 5.50pm an hour after you left the church hall. I think you waited in the car park for Sandra de Villiers then attacked her?

Then you went home to New Marsh to get changed because you were covered in Sandra's blood." DCI Barnes went for the throat. *The detectives knew they had no solid evidence that he had done anything wrong yet, but they were sure they had their man.*

"No, Sandra de Villiers was a lovely lady I would never do anything like that." Mr Whelan replied strongly, "It was snowing and the roads were getting slippery."

"But it only takes 20 minutes to get from the church to Ravensdale Nursing home."

"I had an accident on Edenfield Road outside the Catholic Primary School. The roads were terribly icy and skiddy. I slipped off the road and hit a post box."

"Can we go and inspect your car for damage?" DS Carruthers interrupted.

"Yes, there are scratches on the front of the car and also my tyre burst. It took me ages to change it. I am not as young as I once was. It was bitterly cold and I had forgotten my gloves."

"I don't believe you Mr Whelan." DCI Barnes bent forwards on his chair.

"I'm telling you the truuuth." Mr Whelan stammered.

"Me and DS Carruthers have been looking at your criminal record and its interesting reading. As a minor you were charged with rape of a fellow minor. In 2010 you were charged with DWP and insurance fraud. And most recently you have been charged twice with curb crawling. So, you have a chequered past.

"What has this got to do with the case, his offences were over ten years ago?" Mr Wade defended his client.

"But his curb crawling offences were more recent. Does your younger girlfriend know about them?" Mr Whelan looked vacant.

"I take that's a no Mr Whelan!!!" DCI Barnes grinned.

"We are trying to build a picture of what happened on Friday 16th December 2016." DS Carruthers said, "And Mr Whelan past suggests he's a good liar and cannot be trusted that's why we are questioning him about journey back to the nursing home?"

"What are you not telling us Mr Whelan?" DS Carruthers changed the tone of her voice.

"Mr Whelan times getting on and I'm sure you will be wanting to get to the nursing home to see your mother." Mr Wade had a quiet word with his client.
"I'm telling the truth." Then Mr Whelan threw his arms up and sighed. He was not getting

anywhere fast, he looked at his archaic leather strap wristwatch. He looked defeated.

"I had an accident in my car. Someone ran in front of my car. I thought I had hit someone. We skidded, I ended up on the other side of the road, I collided with a post box and the Primary school railings. I checked my mum and luckily, she was still asleep in the back seat. I got out of the car to check the person who I had hit, they had disappeared. I could not believe there was nobody there. Luckily there was only minor scratches but my front right type had burst because of hitting the curb. It took ages to replace it. It was bitterly cold and it was snowing and like I said before had I forgotten my gloves."

"Who did you hit?" DS Carruthers asked.

"In my head lights, he looked tall, he had long straggly hair, he looked like a vagrant. It happened so quickly then he disappeared. You can come and look at my car. I still have the burst tyre. I did not know if I should report it or not. I was late. I needed to get my mother home."

"We could prosecute you for hit and run, and for leaving the scene of an accident, but there was no injured party and it had been snowing heavily. We will come back to this at a later date!...You are now are free to go home and we

will come and have a look at your car tomorrow."
"Thank you." Mr Wade added. He looked at his client who looked relived.

Mr Whelan and his solicitor made their way out of the building. The detectives went back to the incident room everyone was beavering away at their desks. At the end of the shift, they all went for a well-earned drink at the Stag Inn. It rounded off, a very interesting few days.

It was 5.40pm. The Stag Inn was a stone's throw away from the Police Station. It was its normal charming self. It had ripped brown leather seating, beer glass-stained rickety tables and odd old chairs, archaic wallpaper and distressed paintwork. The bar had a good selection of guest and draught beers. Vintage Christmas songs were played on the pub's sound system. Nobody complained Marion and Keith ran a down and out boozer but they filled it with love and humour. Luckily, they gave it it's character. DCI Barnes brought everyone a drink and Marions assorted cobs were handed around to everyone to munch on, they went down a treat. DS Carruthers sat talking to DC Kapoor and DS Read. DS Read was in his early fifties, 6 foot, thickset, he had a sweeping moustache, olive skin and thick black hair going grey at the temples. Duncan always smelled of polo's mints because he was trying his best to pack up smoking. He had a dry sense of humour, but he had to have, he supported the gunners to the disgruntlement of his fellow colleagues. DCI Barnes called for quiet in the pub.

"As you all know DS Read is back with us after two weeks at our national training college. You will all be happy to know he has just been appointed DI and is taking over from DI Love who is retiring on Christmas Eve." Everyone clapped and cheered.

"You kept that quiet. DS Read." DS Carruthers said quietly. *She felt a bit jealous as she had gone for promotion as well.*

"Well done…You will make a fine Detective Inspector." DC Kapoor interjected and shook his hand.

As he sat there, he was congratulated by all the team. At one point he had three doubles of his favourite whiskey on the table. All the team drank into the night most of them joined in with the karaoke. At the end of the night the detectives rang for taxis because they all had too much to drink, but this was par for the course for a Saturday night.

CHAPTER NINE
Sunday 18th December

The incident room was a cacophony of noise this morning. DS Carruthers was not in a great mood, she had a banging head. When she got home from the Stag Inn she continued drinking and polished off a bottle of Southern Comfort. DC Kapoor was his normal chatty self in the car on the way in. DS Carruthers bit his head off and told him to shut-up. The rest of the journey was silent, but when they arrived at the police station carpark, she apologised profusely to him. He was her work partner and probably the only real friend she had at the Serious Crime Unit.

The briefing did not take long this morning. The Senior officers sat at the front while the detective constables sat behind them. DCI Barnes stood at the evidence board, pen in hand waving it like he was conducting his orchestra.

"Good morning, folks…Now I'm not an alarmist, but uniformed, control- room staff and my wife's forensic team and now DC Brookes are coming down with sickness and diarrhoea and are dropping like flies. That's why the post-mortem is late I have been reassured we will have them first thing in the morning. All of you please sanitise your hands frequently with the hand sanitiser dotted around the departments. We can't cope with a full-scale outbreak all departments are over stretched as it is. I do have some forensics results? All the fingerprints and blood found at the crime scene was from the victim Sandra de Villiers. There were no traces of blood found at the Sandra's home. The blood on the antique dagger was the victims, no finger prints. DNA samples that were taken at the crime scene, house and the murder weapon won't be with us for a while yet. Two laptops, tablets, Johan's mobile phone, an office pc were seized by SOCO they are now being analysed by the Tech department. DC Matthews and DC Booth are still looking at hours of CCTV footage…Last night at 9pm. Mr Barry Eccles from 22 Gorton Road handed in Sandra de Villiers red leather bag. Inside was her iPhone and an empty purse. He found it in his front garden. Sergeant Mills at the front desk put it in a forensic bag and arranged for Mr Eccles to have his fingerprints taken and sent the handbag to forensics. We will hopefully expect the results today or tomorrow morning."

"Are we assuming it's a man guv?" DC Kapoor enquired.

"Forensics are looking at the boot treads, make, model and size etc. Again, we will have the results tomorrow. So, we are open to the fact that they could be from a woman, but if you look at the treads on the evidence board the tread indicates that they had very broad feet. But again, you never know they could be a red herring to direct us in the wrong direction. That's what I have so far...DS Carruthers and DC Kapoor I want you to go to Mr Eccles house on Gorton Road and see if he has any CCTV cameras and knows anything else that can help us? DC Dempster and DC Windass. I want you to go to New Marsh and look at Charlie Whelan's car. Let's see if he is telling the truth? OK folks get to it." He clapped his hands loudly.

DC Kapoor found the roads around the Town centre dirty and slushy. The unmarked police car turned into Church Street and passed the crime scene. It looked like nothing horrific had taken place. DC Kapoor drove on to Gorton Road, it was void of cars. He parked the unmarked police car at the bottom of Mr Eccles driveway, half on the road half on the pavement. DC Kapoor squeezed out and DS Carruthers waited for a blue French-made car to pass before she got out. DS Carruthers shivered from head to toe. She had forgotten her woollen scarf. It was probably on the back of her chair in the incident room. The sky was deepening it's blue minute by minute even though the winter sun had made an appearance it remained chilly. The detectives unbolted the black double wrought iron gates and walked up the sloping driveway.

DC Kapoor rapped loudly on the unforgiving hard wooden door but nobody seemed at home. He stepped back and pointed to a CCTV camera then he turned away and was violently sick on the patchy snow-covered drive. DS Carruthers hammered on the door but still no response. She left a card for the occupants to ring the Serious Crime Unit when they returned home. A girl in her late teens with short brown hair, who smelled of cigarettes, appeared over the dividing tall fence. The detectives flashed their Police warrants in her face.

"Mr and Mrs Eccles have gone away for Christmas. They have gone to their son's, in Newcastle. They will be coming back before the end of December. They throw a great New Year's party." The girl chuckled. The detectives thanked her and disappeared down the driveway towards the unmarked police car.

"Why was you sick?" DS Carruthers asked.

"Don't know, I feel, ok?" DC Kapoor replied.

"I hope you're not coming down with that mystery bug."

When DS Carruthers got in the car her mobile rang in her duffle coat. It was DCI Barnes. She told him about the findings at Mr Eccles house.

"Damn things are moving slower than expected, their CCTV coverage could be vital to this investigation, and we have to wait until the end of December." DCI Barnes replied, he was very annoyed, "I have just spoken to Sergeant Ross. Uniformed are going to do another house to house this afternoon. A lot of people were out when they last visited and there's been no luck with the leaflets."

"Ok, Guv. Me and DC Kapoor are calling at McDonald's on the way back, do you want anything?"

"Yes me, DI Love and DI Read will have a large big mac each."

"OK. Guv." She ended the call.

SAME TIME, SAME PLACE.

DC Windass and DC Dempster had been paired together a lot this year. It was a combination of DC Windass's brawn and DC Dempster's intellect. They both knew Stowgarth and the surroundings area like the back of their hands. Aswell as being work colleagues they were good friends. Most Sunday afternoons when they were not on-call they would have a round of golf at the prestigious Grayson Golf Club. They had been nominated for their private membership by DI Love. He was on the membership committee. Occasionally they would bump into him in the 19th

hole with his pals half sozzled. DC Windass was fantastic on the driving range, and he teed off beautifully, DC Dempster was not as strong but he had a better technique around the greens. So, they were evenly matched.

DC Windass drove them to the New Marsh area of town. The houses were all ex-council and were now privately owned. Most of them had been turned into rental accommodation, two and three properties, flats and bedsits.

Mr Whelan lived in his mum's house on Teddington Terrace. The paintwork on the window frames and front door were distressed looking; they were crying out for a fresh coat of paint. The net curtains in the living room window had seen better days; they were old, dirty and worn. The detectives looked apprehensive of what the inside looked like. Mr Whelan answered the door, he was wearing a burgundy woollen jumper that was far too big for him and khaki trousers.

"Have you come to see my car?" He said slowly and softly. You could tell he was a little drunk.

"Follow me, I will get my keys to the garage." The detectives followed him through a room that was supposed to be the living room. It was dark and drab and it was full of cardboard boxes.

There were piles of clothes, books and newspapers.

The house had a severe damp problem. The smell was atrocious. There was an old ripped blue three-piece suite next to the dining room window and a small table. On top was a small radio, a bottle of pills of some description and half a bottle of Irish Whiskey and a half empty glass. They made their way into a paved backyard where they were greeted by two well looked after solid black Staffordshire bullterriers. The detectives were thankful for the fresh unpolluted air.

"Don't worry about them, they are both soft but they look the part." Mr Whelan laughed. The two young female dogs fought for their attention; they were both lively and mischievous. The garage backed onto the houses opposite. Mr Whelan unlocked the rusty padlock on the garage door.

"I have been drinking, can I drive the car forward so you can look at it?" Mr Whelan asked.

"I will drive it forward." DC Windass frowned. He jumped inside the silver car and drove it out into the daylight. DC Dempster examined the car. He had definitely had a collision with something. The front wing and bumper had been dented and traces of red paint had been left behind. Charlie showed them the burst tyre from the boot of the car. DC Dempster took some pictures on his mobile phone.

"Where did you have the accident?" DC Windass asked. Mr Whelan explained where and what happened on Friday night. The detectives assumed he was telling the truth, but they decided to visit the scene of the accident.

CHAPTER TEN

Edenfield Road was only thirty minutes away from New Marsh. They had to drive through the town centre but luckily the traffic was not busy. The detectives arrived at their destination. They parked on the opposite side of the road to the post box and the Catholic Primary School railings. Large flakes of snow started falling from the sky. The detectives trudged over the road in the wet slush. The railings had been dented and silver paint from Charlies Whelan's car was left behind on the post box for all to see. There had definitely been a collision.

DC Dempster again took some photos on his mobile phone. These photos and the one's of Mr Whelan's car would prove that he was telling the truth about the accident. But the assigned department would deal with him about his hit and run accident. They returned to the unmarked police vehicle; an elderly woman was standing by the unmarked police car.

"Are you the police?" She asked.

"Yes, love." DC Windass replied.

"Are you both here about the accident on Friday night?"

The detectives said yes, and they asked the

elderly woman if she had anything to tell them. She nodded and the detectives asked her to take a seat in the warmth of the car. So, they could take a statement.

"My name is Mrs Stadler. I live at that house with blue painted door." She pointed out the car window. Mrs Stadler looked to be in her late seventies. She had white hair spilling over a moon shaped face and false teeth, yellow tobacco stained, they need bleaching. She wore large oversized glasses over light caramel eyes. She wore an old grey coat and pink jogging bottoms. Mrs Stadler collaborated Mr Whelan's story. She was watching a well-known drama series on television when she heard the bang outside. She looked out the window and a silver car had smashed into the post-box and school railings. Because of the heavy snow the phone line was not working and she did not own a mobile phone so she could not phone the police. She could not go and see if the person was alright because she was not fantastic on her legs and she was frightened of falling.

Anyway, she continued watching her television programme. She looked out her window and the car had disappeared. DC Windass took her statement and thanked her for all her help. DC Dempster helped her out the car and walked her to her door safely. Mrs Stadler asked him to wait a minute and disappeared inside. She reappeared with an old Tupperware box full of freshly made mince pies. DC Dempster was overwhelmed with the gesture. He went back to the car, and they sped off in the direction of the police station.

DS Carruthers and DC Kapoor carried two pizza boxes into the police station.

The lift was full of newbies, but they managed to squeeze in. They were on a guided tour of the building and outside facilities.

When they reached the second floor DC Dimka was stood waiting for the lift.

"Hiya Serg, Johan de Villiers has come in to formally identify his wife's body. So, I'm on my way to reception to collect him and take him down to the mortuary department."

"Thanks, let me know how it goes?"

"Ok, Serg."

The afternoon shift was uneventful there had been two enquiries earlier and nothing led to the killer. At the end of the shift a handful of detectives joined DS Carruthers and DC Kapoor at the Stag Inn.

DS Carruthers drank lager out of the bottle

and had always had a whiskey chaser. She stood at the fruit machine talking to DC Kapoor. He didn't drink alcohol; orange juice was his choice of refreshment.

"When are you supposed to be getting married?" DS Carruthers asked.

"Not until March 2017." DC Kapoor stated.

"Have you had many serious relationships?" DS Carruthers enquired.

"Not really…just one-night stands."

"When was your last one?" DS Carruthers probed further.

"Regrettably, recently, it was a one-night stand, it wasn't all about sex we had a connection. I am hoping this does not affect my marriage to Chadda."

"You have now tasted forbidden fruit." DS Carruthers wagged her finger in front of his face.

"I'm only getting married because it's an arranged marriage. She's a lovely girl, but I don't think I can be true to her and my family." DC Kapoor said.

"I am sure you will make the perfect husband." DS Carruthers loved joking with him.

DCI Barnes came over to speak to her, "Can I have a word?" He moved towards the other end of the bar. Out of the way of flapping ears. DS Carruthers followed him.

"I am watching how much you are drinking. I don't mind you drinking but take it easy. I expect Senior Officers to set an example."

"Sorry, Guv." DS Carruthers apologised, curtsied and licked his boots.

When DS Carruthers finished her latest drink she went to the bar. She decided to have a long glass of coke with plenty of ice. She bent over the bar and asked Marion to put a sly double in it. Marion and DS Carruthers shared a cheeky smile. Luckily no one seemed any the wiser.

The rest of the evening was great. A male duo tribute band had taken to the small stage. They were really good and everyone knew their songs.

The music brought back memories of DS Carruthers school disco days. DC Kapoor was tired so DS Carruthers told him to go home, and she would get a taxi home. Only a few detectives stayed until the end. DS Carruthers was going straight home, but she was starving. She asked the taxi driver to take her to her local kebab house in Cheadley Heath. It was not far from her home on Ivy Street.

The black cab pulled into Ivy Street. DS 'Faith' Carruthers paid the fare and staggered out of the car. The street was dimly lit by lamp posts and her house has expected was in total darkness. She rented a three-bedroom house, it was too big for her, but it came with the job and the rent was very low compared to rental properties in the surrounding area. DS Carruthers opened the white UPVC front door and put the light on. She was blinded by the hallway light. She lost her balance and fell against the magnolia woodchip wall. Faith sat in a heap on the burgundy-red inexpensive cord carpet, it spread through the house except for the kitchen and bathroom. She had drunk far too much; she should never have stayed until the end of the tribute act. Faith slept where she had fallen, it might have only been about twenty minutes. She woke-up and wondered where she was, her head was thumping hard. The shish kebab lay unopened beside her. She dragged herself to her feet and staggered to the galley kitchen.

She saw something in the corner of her eye. It made her jump. It was her feline friend 'PICKLES.' He was a big fat ginger tom. Faith loved him, he was getting on now. He was ten years old. She had rehomed him from a local cat shelter in Bedford when he was 9 weeks old. He had been found in a skip with five other siblings. Faith chose him because he was the only male kitten there.

Pickles was pleased to see his mum. In its claws was a small golden-brown dormouse. Faith could see it was dead. She ushered him into the dining room. She did not want to see him devouring his prey. Faith put the light on, she wanted to make herself a cup instant coffee preferably black with three sugar cubes. She felt something harsh gritty under foot, it was broken shards of glass. The back door had been smashed in and was wide open, for a minute she did not know what to do. She was a Detective Sergeant, but she was rooted to the spot. She felt for her mobile phone. She called the only friend she had, DC 'Vikram' Kapoor. He told her to ring the station and he was on his way. Faith thanked him dearly.

It did not take DC Kapoor long to get to Ivy Street. He found Faith sitting on the doorstep chuffing away on a cigarette and guzzling from a bottle of wine.

"Whoever it was, they long gone?" Faith announced.

"Anything taken?" Vikram asked.

"Strangely enough, nothing." The detectives looked puzzled.

A patrol car with two uniformed officers arrived at Faith's house. They walked around the house and the surrounding streets. Faith did not want it taken any further, but she wanted it recording. The uniformed officers received an urgent request to respond to an assault at the Nero's Nightclub in Stowgarth Town Centre. They left the scene quick as lightning. Faith stood on the front doorstep, she thought she saw someone steering in her direction from the end of the street. She looked again, but they had gone.

"Faith, would you like me to stay until morning?" Vikram interrupted.

"No, I could not ask you to do that."

"I don't mind, I am still living with my parents. They won't even notice I am not there."

Vikram made himself comfortable on the sofa. Faith brought him a single duvet and a pillow.

"It gets quite cold down here, the heating normally comes on about 6am, but I have put it on now."

"Thanks Faith."

Faith was glad of the company. She took some paracetamols and went to bed. Vikram was wide awake as he lay surfing the net on his mobile phone. Suddenly out of the blue it bleeped, he had received a text from Faith. That was odd because she was only upstairs in bed.

ARE YOU AWAKE? DO YOU FANCY A COFFEE? I NEED TO SPEAK TO YOU. Vikram frowned and texted OK.

Faith appeared in a short black lace lingerie and a knitted woollen cardigan with two cups of coffee. She turned the tall lamp on by the lounge window. Vikram was in awe, her legs were long, smooth and very sexy. He could not look at her straight in the eye. She lay with her legs up on the opposite two-seater red draylon sofa smoking a cigarette.

"What did you want to talk to me about?" Vikram was inquisitive.

"I don't know how to start; you can tell anyone." Faith sounded vulnerable; a side Vikram had never seen before.

"You know I left Norwich CID, and I was transferred here. Well, I lied I was transferred from the Luton CID. My husband 'Ronnie' Ronald Carruthers was charged with rape and attempted murder."

"Who was the victim?" Vikram asked softly. Faith was physically trembling.

"Me." She burst into a flood of tears.

Vikram beckoned her to him; he opened the duvet and she climbed inside. Faith put her arms around him and cried. Vikram wrapped his warm strong, safe arms around her. When she stopped crying, they lay talking.

"It's supposed to be under wraps, me coming here." Faith was clearly upset.

"Does DCI Barnes know anything about your husband?"

"Yes, he knows the reason for my transfer, but nobody else knows except Detective Chief superintendent Hargreaves."

"Do you think it's your husband?" Vikram enquired.

"He's on remand at HMP Bedford. We go to trial on Monday 16th March 2017…He's probably sent one of his cronies to frighten me."

"Was your husband a copper?"

"Yes, he was a detective inspector in Luton CID but they dismissed him and he blames me for losing his job and his liberty. There was a chance he was going to come out on bail, so I packed up my things and stayed with my sister and her family in Norwich. Then I was transferred here." Faith said. Vikram wrapped his bulging arms around her tighter, his hairy chest was beating harder than before. He wanted to know more, but she would tell him in her own time.

"Thank you." Faith smiled.

"It's ok, nothing will come from me."

Surprisingly they kissed, tenderly at first then passionately. Vikram took off his boxer shorts and lifted up her lace lingerie. The sex was very hot and went on a lot longer than they both anticipated. Afterwards they fell asleep in each other's arms.

CHAPTER ELEVEN
**Earlier that evening.
Sunday 18th December 2016
9pm.**

Two friends were having dinner at their favourite Lebanese Restaurant and Lounge Bar. It was owned by a local wealthy Lebanese family. It was off the High Street in Stowgarth Town centre. It was a stand-alone brick building. It had once been 'R.D Williams Furniture Store.' They moved to a bigger building on the Stowgarth Retail Park on the edge of town some years ago.

The old furniture store had an extensive renovation and refurbishment. The restaurant and the lounge bar had been named 'Jamil.' The name meant beautiful in Lebanese. The restaurant was lavish inside, it had rich sensuous surroundings with a fully licensed bar, a comfy lounge and a middle eastern dining experience.

The two friends had sat at the same table every Sunday evening for the last twenty-four months. It looked on to the High Street. Cody Scott loved to people watch. He continually bitched about what people looked like and what they were wearing. That was one of his many flaws. Cody Scott was an enormous character, loud, outlandish and very gay. He was born and lived in Melbourne,

Australia until he was 21. He moved over to England and settled in Lincolnshire. Cody Scott started working for Stowgarth FM and he had been at the radio station for the last twelve years. He was Stowgarth FM's stalwart disc-jockey. He worked the breakfast show 6am until 10 am and the evening show 5pm until 9pm Monday to Friday. Cody Scott did not work weekends at the radio station. He tried to relax at home, but he often DJ'd at wedding receptions or birthday parties on Saturday nights. Cody Scott was quite the local celebrity and he loved the attention. He was 6foot2 and stocky. In his youth he had a trim physique; he had swimming trials with the Australian Commonwealth Swimming Team, but it did not come to fruition. Cody Scott had blond wavy shoulder length hair, he was tanned, ocean blue eyes and a goatee beard. He was a good-looking guy, but his gob let him down at times. He was wearing blue denim jeans and a burgundy Paul Smith woollen jumper. A brown suede jacket hung on the back of the chair.

Hugo Molinari is Cody Scott's faithful friend of ten years. They had met at the launch party of his first Italian Restaurant in St Enoch's. Hugo Molinari was a local entrepreneur, he had two other restaurants in Stowgarth and Lincoln. He ran a very successful Dance School in Grayson for children and adults of all ages. Dancing was his passion. He taught ballroom, Latin, old time and contemporary dancing. In 1996 Hugo Molinari and his twin sister

Adraina were British Ballroom and Latin Champions. Hugo Molinari was 34 years old. He was tall and slender, but of late he had put some unwanted weight on. Hugo Molinari had Mediterranean olive skin, dark hair shaved around the sides and spiky on top. He wore black graphite glasses over brown oval eyes. Hugo Molinari wore solid gold jewellery and designer labelled clothing.

Cody Scott filled their flute glasses with their favourite sparkling prosecco.

"What kind of week have you had?" Cody Scott asked.

"DON'T GO THERE." He spat out.

"What's up mate?"

"Sorry it's this bloody divorce. It's costing me a bloody fortune. Angelina is not just happy with the marital home in Grayson she now wants piece of my restaurant empire. I'm pot-less Cody. I'm having to have to sell my restaurants in Stowgarth and Lincoln. I'm hanging with grim death on to my restaurant in St Enochs. As you know, you were there, I opened it in 2006 with my parents."

"I thought you had money put aside that your mother and father had left you?" Cody enquired.

"That was spent on the house I brought for our marital home; furniture, furnishings then there were the expensive holidays to the Maldives and cruising around the Caribbean."

"Yes, you spoiled Angelina…I know she is the mother to your twin boys, but she was never the maternal type."

"No that's probably why she had an affair with the instructor from her gym class. They are now living together in our family home."

"Are you still living with your boys at your Dance School?"

"Yes, luckily the warehouse building has three huge floors. The first and second is for the dance school, but I don't use the second floor as much as I used too. I bought the building ten years ago, but I never got around to completely renovating and developing the top floor. My initial idea was to rent it out to a professional person. I never thought I would be living it with my two boys. Luckily, it's in a liveable condition, but it still needs plenty of work and that costs money I haven't got. The boys love the open plan living, but I am not finding it easy. The only time I get to myself is when the boys go to bed then I put my feet up and end up falling asleep in front of the television."

"Oh mate." Cody leaned across the table and touched his arm, "Well I said on the phone, you have helped me out on many occasions, and I don't mind paying for the meal. It's the only real time you get to come out on your own, you are normally working or looking after the boys."

"Thank you." Hugo Molinari smiled.

The Lebanese food came to the table. The waitress was Assi, the owner's beautiful daughter. The food was piping hot, the two men had their usuals. Cody Scott had chicken mezza and Hugo Molinari had lamb mezza. They shared numerous side dishes, the falafel was light, there were mountains of fresh salad, sprouted hummus, rice pilaf and spiced mushrooms. The two friends silently tucked into their meal.

"I know you are having problems with money, but you look bloody awful mate." Cody Scott went straight to the point. He could see he was not his usual chirpy self; he was normally bubbly and chatty.

"I had a disturbing phone call from the husband of a woman who works for me. She was found murdered in her car outside Stowgarth Catholic Church on Friday night."

"Oh mate, that's terrible. Do I know her?"

Cody asked.

"Yes, you have met her at our presentation nights. She used to teach on Wednesday and Thursday evenings. You could not miss Sandra de Villiers. She was the red head, tall and very attractive. You could always hear Sandra de Villiers before you saw her?"

"A bit like me you mean." Cody sniggered into his glass of prosecco, "Yes, I know who you mean. Her husband is my dentist Johan de Villiers. He has a practice here in Stowgarth and he has just opened one in Trussington Village."

"To be honest it has hit me harder than I thought, she was a lovely friend and a fantastic dance teacher. Sandra de Villiers was loved by all her pupils. She will be sadly missed." Hugo Molinari sighed.

"I've heard nothing on the news?" Cody Scott rubbed his hands with delight. He loved to be the first to air breaking local news, but his friend urged him not to reveal the victim's name because her name had not been released by the Police just yet.

They both ate traditional Nummoora (Semolina slices topped with almonds, drizzled in warm syrup) for dessert.

The food was amazing as usual. When they had finished eating they moved from their table and sat down in the lavish and spacious lounge bar. It had a relaxing ambience that was very popular with its clients. The seating was soft brown leather bucket chairs. They sat facing each other. In the background modern Arab music was being played. The owner's daughter came over with another bottle of sparkling prosecco and placed it on the dark wooden table between them.

"Who is the artist being played?" Cody Scott asked.

"It's the king of romance Wael Kfoury, do you like his music?" She replied excitedly.

"Yes, he's very good."

Hugo Molinari this time played mother and filled the flutes with more alcohol. The two friends talked over an hour and drank another bottle of their tipple. Cody Scott did not get drunk he just got louder and louder. Hugo Molinari knew it was time to make tracks. Just before leaving Cody as promised paid the bill in full. He gave the girl six crisp twenty-pound notes and told her to keep the change. The taxi arrived promptly, it took Cody back to his apartment in Cheadley Heath then the taxi cut through the Halstead Estate and dropped Hugo Molinari at the Dance School in Grayson.

CHAPTER TWELVE
7am.

Faith woke-up on the sofa alone. She shouted for Vikram; his clothes had gone from the wicker chair. She peeped through her curtains, but Vikram's car had gone. She called his mobile phone, but it went straight to voice mail. Faith assumed he had gone home with his head lowered in shame. She phoned for taxi she ordered it for 7.40am. She just hoped and prayed there was no much traffic. Faith went for a hot shower. She got out the cubicle and dried herself on a warm fluffy towel off the heated rail.

Faith yawned and stretched in front of the full-length mahogany mirror, her big brown eyes looked red and puffy. She wore a black trouser suit and an ivory blouse and a pair of black flat sensible shoes.

Faith ran downstairs and nearly fell over 'Pickles' who was sat on the bottom step. She hurried into the kitchen. Vikram had brushed up the broken glass and put the fold up wooden table against the back door to secure it. She opened a fresh brown loaf from the wooden bread bin and popped in two slices into the toaster. She filled a bowl with some sub-standard European muesli that she had brought from one of the foreign supermarkets. She had to add a lot sugar to make it edible. She drowned it with full fat milk. She impatiently waited for her toast, she made herself a cup of South American freeze-dried instant coffee and three sugar cubes.

Pickles had followed her into the kitchen. He jumped onto the marble work surface. Faith fed him his favourite cat food and complete biscuits. Faith looked at her mobile phone, she slurped her coffee and quickly ate her cereal. She adorned her black duffle coat and her black woollen scarf and matching gloves. A taxi beeped from outside. She rushed out the door with a slice of toast in one hand and her mobile phone in the other.

Stowgarth was under a thick blanket of fog. The snow was relentless. The roads were treacherous due to the plummeting conditions. The traffic was a choka this morning. There had been a collision between a yellow and car and a gigantic haulage truck. Stowgarth Town Centre was too small for large trucks, because the roads were too narrow and bendy. When it was market day they could only just cope with the influx of traffic and visitors. The local councillors knew it was an on-going problem, but the sitting council could never get a majority to pass the changes.

Traffic police, paramedics and a fire engine were at the scene of the tailback snaked around the one-way system causing everyone to come to a complete halt. The taxi was stuck, the driver had no way of changing direction and finding a better way to their destination. Faith realised they were not going to get anywhere to fast. She texted DCI Barnes: SORRY BOSS. THERE'S A BAD ACCIDENT ON THE ONE-WAY SYSTEM. I WILL BE WITH YOU AS SOON AS THE TRAFFIC CLEARS. DS Carruthers.

The taxi driver turned on the local Radio station, 'STOWGARTH FM.' A song was being played. Faith and the driver sang along.

The Aussie DJ Cody Scott announced the local News headlines.

"On Friday evening there was a murder in the Stowgarth Catholic Church car park. A local woman Sandra de Villiers was the unfortunate victim. Her family and friends have been left devastated….There's been another armed robbery at a local off-license on the Halstead Estate. This also took place on Friday evening. The police are still no wiser who the armed robbers are. Nobody was hurt, but plenty taken…If anyone knows or seen anything about the murder or the armed robberies don't hesitate to ring Stowgarth Police Station or email me at (cody.scott@stowgarthfm.com) and I will pass on your confidential information." He ended the local news headlines. DS Carruthers thought *Well, he was quick to get his information. I will mention it at the briefing.* DS Carruthers mobile phone bleeped. She retrieved it from her winter coat. YOUR NOT THE ONLY ONE WHO IS STUCK IN THE TRAFFIC. THE BRIEFING WILL TAKE PLACE WHEN YOU ALL GET HERE. – She replaced it in her pocket and waited for the traffic to move.

DCI Barnes started the briefing an hour later than scheduled.

"Glad you are all here safe and sound, another accident on the town's one-way system. Well, I finally have the post-mortem results, this mystery bug is causing mayhem. That's why everything is being delayed. We have had DC Brookes and DC Kapoor phone in sick this morning." DCI Barnes sighed, then continued. "Sandra had twelve deep stab wounds in her abdomen and chest. She had numerous defence wounds on her hands and arms. She had not been sexually assaulted, but she was six weeks pregnant. There were no fingerprints found on the murder weapon, but we did find fibres on the handle. The killer wore black woollen gloves like millions of people in Great Britain at this time of the year. Someone was very careful or very lucky. We all know the toxicology results are going to take 4 to 6 weeks…"

DCI Barnes asked everyone to gather around the nearest office desk and everyone watched the laptop.

"What have we got DC Matthews?" DCI Barnes asked. Detective Constables Matthews was in his late thirties, he looked butch, but he was as camp as a row of tents. He had short blond cropped hair and a forces style parting. He had pale blue eyes under blue graphite spectacles. DC Matthews had a well-groomed beard. His arms were covered in oriental designed tattoo's. He had been working in the Serious Crime Unit for about 12 years. He joined them from the Cambridgeshire Police Force. Five years ago, he had a terrible motorbike accident. DC Matthews was relegated to the wheelchair, but he adapted well. He had a sound sharp mind and he was a highly intelligent individual. He made computer support one of the most important resources in the Serious Crime Unit. He worked closely with DC Booth.

"On Saturday afternoon at 3.45pm, we found Sandra's red estate car traveling down the A2580 between Trussington and Stowgarth. 20 minutes later she is spotted entering the town centre. She drives around the one-way system on to the high street then she turns on to church street. That's when the towns CCTV camera's lose her. That part of town is not covered by cameras. We assume she parks her vehicle in the church carpark at 4.05pm."

DC Matthews said.

"We have a witness statement from Mr Whelan the church warden. That Sandra took a seat beside him at the back of the church hall. Mr Whelan says she was about ten minutes late." DC Dimka interrupted.

"Between 3.50pm and 5.30pm we checked the CCTV footage for pedestrians and cars going in and out of church street, nothing looked suspicious, but I do have a list of car registrations. The man Mr Whelan described slipping and sliding along church street was seen on our camera's walking from the direction of the train station. He joined the high street and then turned on to church street at about 4.50pm." DC Matthews continued.

"DC Matthews can you get a close-up on his face?" DCI Barnes interrupted. The green and canary yellow woolly hat was disguising his face.

"This man could be our killer; did he await around to text Sandra de Villiers? Did he lure her to her death? At the press conference tomorrow. We can open it up to the general public. We can ask if this person has been seen walking past the catholic church and heading in the direction of Gorton Road. We can ask if anybody saw anybody acting suspicious around the church car park and surrounding areas." DCI Barnes directed. DCI

Barnes went back to the evidence board.

"DC Dempster can you tell the briefing your and DC Windass findings at Mr Whelan's yesterday?" DCI Barnes shouted across the room. DC Dempster stood-up and told everyone what they had found out.

"DC Dimka, have you managed to go through the de Villiers mobile phone records?" DCI Barnes asked.

"There are a few mobile phone numbers that keep on popping up on the de Villiers mobile phone records. I checked on Johan de Villiers mobile phone that was seized with other devices and looked up the number in his contacts, it comes up as ANNABELLE. I checked Sandra's mobile phone that had been handed in by Mr Eccles, and found the number that had occurred regularly on her mobile phone bill. It was saved under the name DANIEL. I'm now waiting for TECH to get back to me with the text messages."

"Well done, DC Dimka." DCI Barnes praised him. There was no doubt that DC Dimka was his favoured pupil. He had tipped the young Nigerian to go on to big things in the Serious Crime Unit. DC Dimka was already swotting for his Sergeant exam and he was primed to take over from Duncan Read now Detective Inspector.

"As you know uniformed did another house to house on Gorton Road and surrounding streets, yesterday. But nobody saw anything. We all know that church street has no residential buildings. The church is opposite a fenced off piece of land that's been acquired for building, but the council have not approved it yet. It's been earmarked as a site for a high brand supermarket....While you stragglers were still in traffic. I was speaking with DC Booth. She contacted a very awkward Johan de Villiers to find out his wife's GP. She eventually found out that Melrose House Health Centre was her medical practice in Trussington Village. DC Booth gave them a ring and arranged to see her GP Dr Judith Hart. She is going later today…"

"She is being let out on the public then?" DC Windass interrupted. The detectives room erupted in laughter.

DC Booth just smiled. She had been working with DC Matthews for 12 months in his computer support section. DC Booth was a strange woman. She was in her late twenties. She had long black hair and pale white skin. DC Booth had black slug-like tattooed eyebrows over chocolate brown eyes. She did not often wear a dress, but if she did, she still wore her black doc martens. She was nick named 'Morticia' out of the Adam's family. She was very reserved and well-liked by her colleagues.

"DCI Barnes, can I interrupt?"

"Yes, DS Carruthers?"

"When I was stuck in traffic, the taxi driver put on the local radio, the DJ Cody Scott announced that there had been a murder at the Catholic Church car park on Friday night and the victim was Sandra de Villiers. I didn't think her name had been released to the general public?"

"Cody Scott is very good at finding things out in and around Stowgarth…Over the years he has been a good source of relevant information, he likes to have his finger on the pulse and likes to announce breaking news…".

"How does he get hold of the information?" DS Carruthers asked.

"Nobody knows…we must have a leak here at the Station, and I know the Chief Super wants to find out who and why?.. Before I forget DC Dimka, do we have the emails and social media accounts for Johan and Sandra de Villiers. If so, can you analyse them ASAP? Because I have a feeling, they will be quite revealing…Anyway, that's all folks for now. You have plenty to get on with." DCI Barnes finished the briefing and walked back to his office.

DS Carruthers walked back to her desk. She rang Mrs Sweeting to arrange a time to question her about the de Villiers. She was going to be at St Francis Church in Trussington Village all day. There was a morning worship service then the parishioners were having a meeting regarding fund raising for a new organ. So, they agreed to meet after the service about 11am.

DS Carruthers asked the detective constables to gather around her desk.

"Because DC Kapoor is sick, I'm going to be working with DC Dempster." DC Dempster's face drained with blood; DC Windass smiled sardonically.

"DC Windass can you go with DC Booth to the GP's, and DC Dimka you have plenty of things to get on with." DS Carruthers turned to DC Dempster.

"We are going to question Mrs Sweeting at 11pm...so between now and then you can write up your statement from yesterday and answer your emails."

DC Dempster looked petrified; he had never partnered her before. DS Carruthers was known for her cut throat attitude, she was forthright, blunt and sarcastic. DC Dempster did not know how to take her. You could not say she was a bad detective sergeant; she was diligent, tenacious and always got good results. DS Carruthers was really liked by her superior officers. She was known for her 'death stare' this made you sweat and go weak at the knees on the spot. This happened when she was angered or she wanted to ask an important question. She expected it right off the bat and no dilly dallying.

DS Carruthers sat at her desk. She missed DC Kapoor presence; he was always a joy to be around. He made her smile even with the arduous of investigations.

DS Carruthers logged into her laptop; she was surprised to see an email from DC Kapoor in her personal box. Her heart missed a beat and she lost her spit. She opened the email with trepidation. It read *Sorry Faith not been in touch, got this mystery bug. I left early this morning because I felt sick. I should have woken you, but you looked so peaceful asleep. When I got home, I couldn't stop throwing up, when my mobile phone fell out my pocket into the toilet. The phone is knackered and I have ordered a replacement online and it will delivered tomorrow by midday. I enjoyed the passionate night together, I was really not expecting that to happen. It was wild and it blew my mind. You are a very foxy lady. I cannot wait for it to happen again. That's if you enjoyed it too. I will hopefully see you at work tomorrow. Thanks Vikram.*

DC Carruthers was chuffed to bits; she had been beating herself over her head that morning. It was nice to be wanted again even though there was about twenty years between them. It might only be occasional sex and she had to take it at face value. DC Kapoor was a lot younger than her and he was getting married to his fiancé Chadda in March next year. Before DS Carruthers got on with the thousand and one emails, she went to the canteen for her breakfast.

CHAPTER THIRTEEN

St Francis Church was only a spit away from where the detectives had parked. DS Carruthers looked at the time on the dashboard of the car. It was 10.45am.

"Do we know what Mrs Sweeting looks like?" DC Dempster broke the long silence.

"We are supposed to be detectives. We will use our common sense." DS Carruthers looked at him like a piece of shit, "We will ask inside the church, somebody is bound to know her."

They got out the car and walked up the spiral path towards the church. The biting wind whipped through the graveyard. DS Carruthers was thankful that she had remembered her green woollen scarf, it hung warmly around her neck.

"The church is of a Norman style, it clearly predates Tudor and Jacobean buildings in the Stowgarth area." DC Dempster said in an intellectual voice

"Where did that come from? Have you swallowed a history book?" DS Carruthers piped-up.

"I passed my GCSE'S at school. I passed an

A-Level in History at college then I went onto university, where I gained an Honours Degree in History and Archaeology." DC Dempster said in an educated voice.

"Why did you become a copper?" DS Carruthers sniggered.

"There were not many jobs out there in my chosen field locally and because of my degree I applied for the Lincolnshire Police and they snapped me up straight away."

"Well, I never knew that Detective Constable." DS Carruthers was intrigued by this finding.

The church looked huge from the outside, it had an imposing bell tower in the middle, a solid nave and a large extension that had been built at the end of the building. It did not take them long to reach the stone arched entrance.

"Churches give me the creeps. They always have since I was a kid."

"They are supposed to have the opposite effect." DS Carruthers laughed.

They went inside the old church. Morning worship was still in progress. A lot of the dark wooden pews were empty. The detectives took a seat at the back of the church. The altar was covered in pristine white cloth, it had a large brass cross in the middle. The lady vicar preached her sermon from a tall wooden pulpit. DS Carruthers looked around at the many magnificent intricate woven tapestries. She also noticed the magnificent stained-glass windows.

Suddenly the Star Wars theme tune came blurting out of DC Dempster's coat pocket. He had forgotten to put his mobile phone on silent. The congregation looked in the detective's direction, their faces were black as thunder. DC Dempster coloured the shade of crimson, he dashed outside to take the call. DS Carruthers had a strict Catholic upbringing, but in her early twenties she decided not to follow the same path as her father and grandmother. She didn't believe in anything anymore, working in the police force, she had seen at first-hand how cruel the world was and if there was a god, he would not let innocent people suffer. She only went to church for weddings, christenings and funerals. She did not really want to be in church this morning, but her job had brought her there. From a Catholic perspective. DS Carruthers thought that the service lacked energy, richness, faith and spirit. It was completely different to the church service she was used too as a teenage girl.

Moments later DC Dempster appeared, he

was cold and wet, snowflakes peppered his black winter coat.

"Sorry Serg, it was Human Resources from the station they wanted my new bank details, so they can pay me at the end of December." He said quietly.

The detectives observed the service until the end. A majority of the congregation made their way into the eastern extension of the church. Tea, coffee and assorted cakes were being served. Everyone was sitting down at chairs and tables chatting. DS Carruthers asked an elderly gentleman who was sitting close to the sliding doors if he knew who Mrs Sweeting was. Unfortunately, he had a bad stammer, he pointed them in the direction of a group of ladies who were sitting at a large wooden oval table. As they approached a small slim lady with steel blue eyes and blue glasses came towards them. Her hair surprisingly had a pink tinge to it, it was thick and full of curls and it touched her shoulders.

"Good morning. We are looking for Mrs Sweeting?" DS Carruthers asked.

"That's me, I assume you are DS Carruthers?" The slim lady said quietly.

"Yes, and this is Detective Constable Dempster." As procedure they both showed their

Police warrant cards. Mrs Sweeting broke away from the group of ladies and they sat at a small wooden table out of ear shot.

"It's nice to put a face to the phone call…It's so sad to hear about Sandra." Mrs Sweeting spoke louder than before.

"When did you first find out about Mrs de Villiers death?" DS Carruthers began her questions. DC Dempster took notes.

"I spoke to Mr de Villiers on the night of his wife's murder. He called me at 10pm. I just started to nod off to sleep in bed. He seemed devastated. He was so upset. I offered to come over, but he said he was better left on his own. He had said he had rung Mrs de Villiers parents in Canada they were devastated and they will be coming over for the funeral."

"How would you describe your relationship with Mrs de Villiers?"

"Fine…I cared for her like I did with her husband. They both have parents who lived abroad. It was more than just housekeeping I looked after them like they were my own family."

"When was the last time you saw Mrs de Villiers?"

"I saw her at the Old Granary on Friday afternoon, I was ironing in the kitchen. It was about 3.30pm. She came and dropped off the dogs then she went straight out to the dance recital."

"What time did you leave Mr de Villiers alone?"

"I left at 4pm."

"Do you know where Mrs de Villiers had been that day?"

"It was the Cambridgeshire Championship Dog Show at the Peterborough Showground. She went with a friend Samantha Mealing. She runs ringcraft training at the Grayson Community Centre. It takes place tomorrow tonight at 6pm."

"Can you think of anybody who would want to harm Mrs de Villiers?"

"No, she was loved by everyone, that's once you got to know her." Mrs Sweeting smiled.

"What do you mean by that?" DS Carruthers probed.

"Mrs Sweeting could be a bit over the top, loud, brash and she did not care who she offended but once you got to know her, you easily fell in love with her."

"How did she seem to you the days leading up to her murder?"

"To be honest she was not her chirpy self, she seemed distant and preoccupied. I just thought she had fallen out with Mr de Villiers. No marriage is without its problems.

"Mr de Villiers said his wife was very secretive at times. Do you know why?"

"No, Mr de Villiers said she retrieved calls and texts at strange hours of the night. Mr de Villiers said she had been late home many times and offered lame excuses. And he was concerned because she was spending more money than usual." Mrs Sweeting had verified what Mr de Villiers had told them.

The snow was falling heavily. The detectives dashed down to the unmarked police car. They were drenched through and freezing cold. DC Dempster scraped the snow away from the front and back windscreens. The detectives drove through the village they joined a couple of cars following a council gritter. It was not long before they were speeding back up the A2580 towards Stowgarth

As soon as DS Carruthers and DC Dempster

arrived back at the police station DS Carruthers went to see DCI Barnes in his office. She told him her findings. DS Carruthers thought she was withholding something from them, but she did not know what.

"Well, you might have to question here again, but here at the station." DCI Barnes said. DS Carruthers looked a little perplexed.

"I have some interesting developments so I have called a briefing." He looked at watch, "In 45 minutes, you might as well go for lunch and take DC Dempster with you."

CHAPTER FOURTEEN

"Thanks to DC Dimka's hard work. He has been looking through the texts from Johan and Sandra's texts, emails and bank accounts…Well where do I start?...Johan de Villiers is having a sexual relationship with ANNABELLE." He pointed to her photo on the evidence board. Annabelle was beautiful she had piercing blue eyes, tanned and long blond hair.

"It was taken on Johan's mobile phone. The texts are romantic and sexual in nature, but there is nothing to suggest they had anything to do with Sandra's murder…Sandra's texts were interesting too, she was meeting up with DANIEL on a regular basis. These were not romantic or sexual in nature. So, we are assuming they are friends. The mobile phone Daniel is using is from a pay as you go and it's not registered to anyone.

"We need to find and speak to Annabelle and Daniel?"

Duncan Read took centre stage as the New Detective Inspector. The detectives cheered and clapped.

"As you know I don't officially take over from DI Love until Christmas Eve, but DCI Barnes wanted me on this murder case and I'm presently co-working with him and DI Love." DI Read paused for a moment.

"We have forensics results on the bloody footprints from the crime scene and Gorton Road. They are from a men's boot, a well-known make, size 9 and they are manufactured in black or light brown leather. Thousands of these are sold daily in the UK and their biggest outlet is on-line...DC Booth and DC Windass went to see Sandra de Villiers General Practitioner. They found out that Sandra had been on Benzodiazepines for insomnia, panic and an anxiety disorder. She had been on them for years. The Dr said her anxiety and panic attacks were increased by the continual infidelity of her husband. She found it hard to sleep at night. The doctor said she had a fertility problem. Having had many miscarriages and she had three IVF treatments, but she still did not conceive. This did not help her depression, she blamed herself that Johan could not have a son or daughter. They were told about her cocaine abuse. The doctor encouraged her to stop because of the effect it was having on her body and health. The GP seems to think she continued to use it because she thought it improved her mood. We will be able to see if there are any drugs in Sandra's body once we get the toxicology results..." DI Read stepped down from centre stage. Another applause from the detectives gathered. DCI Barnes took over again.

"Now I have the long-awaited email and

social media reports thanks. I will start with Sandra's tablet. I found that her social media was used regularly. She used social media all the time. She had regular conversation with her mum and dad in Canada. She had a lot of contact with dog friends and people she taught at the Dance School. Something interesting has come to light. DC Matthews has found who the mystery Daniel is?" DS Carruthers was on tenterhooks smacking her lips in anticipation for the information.

"He is Sandra's brother...There is only one conversation between them. It was posted on Monday 3rd July 2016 at 8pm. The username was Daniel Hardy. He had asked her to be a friend on many occasions before, but she had not added him to her list of friends. But on this occasion, she did. He contacted her without a photograph. Stating he would upload it later but he never does. He explained he was 28 years old and he was born 5 years after Sandra was taken into care and they shared the same parents. Explaining that their parents were both dead. Their father Philip Thorne died aged 50 in 2006 of liver sclerosis and their mother died two years later aged 55 of a heroin overdose. He was taken into care when he 5 years old because his mum and dad were crackheads and they did not look after him properly. He was found malnourished and living in squalor. Sandra replied to his post on the same day at 10pm. Sandra told him it was not safe to talk on social media in case her husband found out. So, she gave him her mobile number and she said she would like to meet-up with him...Now according to our mobile phone texts, he contacted her the next day and they arranged to meet up at the Coffee House in Stowgarth Town Centre on Friday 7th July 2016 at 10.30 am...DC Matthews did some digging this morning online. He searched on the Stowgarth Registration Office Website. He found out that Daniel Thorne was adopted at the age ten and he was renamed Daniel Hardy. Sandra Thorne was adopted at the age of eight and was renamed Sandra Rawlinson and they both grew up and lived in and around Stowgarth...The more we find out the more intriguing this investigation gets?...Regarding Johan's laptop results. He's a busy man. On a personal level he has a lot of conversations with his family South Africa on face book. Being a member of many dating websites which he uses them frequently. A lot of the messaging has sexual content and he arranged meetings with them for sex. Using the holiday hotel in St Enoch's for his liaisons...I will pass you back to DI Read he looked over the de Villiers bank accounts this morning." The senior detectives changed places again.

"I looked at Sandra's own Nationwide bank account. £2000 was transferred into her account every month by her husband. The account was quite healthy up until 2016 then her monthly allowance was starting to be eaten away. She had numerous store and credit cards, all of which had been maxed out. There was £5000 pounds owing on each. I checked Johan's personal and business bank accounts. Mr de Villiers is a very wealthy man. He has over half a million in his personal account, half million in his savings account. The old granary is free from mortgage. His business account is very healthy, but he does have a hefty mortgage on his new dental practice in Trussington. The Stowgarth Practice is free from mortgage....I looked at their email accounts and to be honest Sandra hardly used hers at all. Joahn's was more interesting. He increased his and Sandra's life insurance policy up to a million pounds. This begs the question? Did he pay someone to bump his wife off. But as we can see his by his bank accounts are very healthy. It is pretty safe to say that money is not a motive here. Did he have her murdered so he could move this Annabelle in the marital home...This could be a positive motive...That's all I have now folks." DCI Barnes had a hoarse throat and walked pensively to the coffee machine.

"DS Carruthers, can I have a word?" DCI Barnes beckoned her to him.

"I know you and DC Dempster are going to Grayson tonight to question this Amanda Mealing, but do you think you can go and see Johan de Villiers. There are a lot of unanswered questions. Leave finding Daniel until tomorrow."

"Yes, Guv."

CHAPTER FIFTHTEEN

DC Dempster followed DS Carruthers down to the ground floor and through an empty reception. "Where are we going, Serg?"

"We are going to see Johan de Villiers."

"What about the car?"

"God gave us legs DC Dempster and Stowgarth Dental Practice is in walking distance." DS Carruthers laughed.

The entrance door opened automatically. They confronted the plummeting temperatures outside.

The winter sun was shining low, it was just peeping over the town hall. The sky was full of misshapen clouds and the air was still cold. Most of the snow was now turning into slush. The Christmas tree outside town hall was amazing. The local council had definitely pulled out all the stops this Christmas. The market traders were finishing setting up their stalls. There was also a Grimsby fishmonger and a local butchers van, both of them auctioning off there produce.

The town came to life when it was market day. DS Carruthers received a text, she explained her findings to DC Dempster.

The Stowgarth Dental practice was across the square in the banks old building. It didn't look like a bank anymore. It had undergone a complete face-lift. It was light and airy. There were posh yellow large leather sofas and chairs dotted around sporadically. There was a massive screen televising local businesses and events. There were racks full of up-to-date magazines and there was even a large children's play area.

The receptionist was a beautiful tall young girl. She had short blond hair, immaculate shiny teeth and large watery blue eyes.

"Mr de Villiers is with a patient, but you can go in as soon as he as finished."

"Thank you." DS Carruthers looked at her name badge, "Olivia." DC Dempster looked embarrassed, but the receptionist didn't seem bothered.

Next to the reception was a wall full of staff photographs. DC Dempster pointed out Annabelle Wolfe she was a dental nurse at the practice.

15 Minutes later, a grey-haired man appeared from Room 4. He was holding his face in discomfort. The receptionist looked across at the

detectives, they were already entering Room 4.

Johan de Villiers was sat at a computer screen, he didn't even look in their direction.

"Mr de Villiers." DS Carruthers said in a high octave voice. She took a seat facing him while DC Dempster stood beside her.

"We have a lot of unanswered questions?"

Johan laughed, 'I'm busy, can't it wait, I have a patient in five minutes. My receptionist should not have let you through."

"Like I said to your receptionist, I reminded her that we are officers of law and it is a murder investigation…And I'm sure Mr de Villiers you want us to catch the person who murdered your wife.

"How did you know I was here?"

"Well, it did not take much working out Mr de Villiers?" DS Carruthers said in sarcastic tone.

"So here we are Mr de Villiers." DC Dempster interrupted. DS Carruthers smiled. It was the first time that DC Dempster had met Johan de Villiers and his arrogant personality preceded him.
"I take it you haven't come with any good

news?" Johan said sarcastically.

"We have found your wife's red leather bag, purse and mobile phone. The DNA and fingerprints were your wife's and there were no other traces….Does the name DANIEL mean anything to you." DS Carruthers announced.

"No, I have never heard of him."

"Well, it's a good job we know who he is?" DS Carruthers said proudly.

She told him who he was, and his relationship to his wife.

"I only knew that Sandra was fostered by the Rawlinson's she was totally neglected by her biological parents. She stayed with them until she was eventually adopted. Brian was an English teacher at the Catholic Grammar in St Enochs. Sandra had a very stable loving relationship with her parents."

"Why did you increase yours and Sandra's life insurance's to a million pound?" DS Carruthers continued.

"Well, we know you couldn't have killed your wife, but did you arrange someone else to do your dirty work., Mr de Villiers?" DC Dempster interjected abruptly. He knew by interrupting it was making Johan think harder and quicker.

"No!" Johan fumed. He bit his clenched fist in temper.

"Calm down! Mr de Villiers?" DC Dempster snapped.

"I'm a rich man and I was worried if anything happened to me that she wouldn't be able to have the lifestyle she has now…I married Sandra when I was 21. She worked at my first practice in Carnaby Street, but when I was making big bucks. I promised she could have a good lifestyle…She took her teachers exam in Ballroom and Latin dancing and she followed her dream. Showing, breeding and judging Golden Retrievers and she did that to the best of her ability. OK, I showered her with money, that was because I loved her." Johan had calmed down.

"We have spoken with the pathologist, Sandra was six weeks pregnant." DS Carruthers said delicately.

"WHAT!!!" He put his face in his hands. He tried to compose himself, he said,

"She had many miscarriages and IVF treatments, with no success…So was she cheating on me with someone else." Johan's temper rose again. He couldn't understand why Sandra was six weeks pregnant. He knew it could not be his."

"We'd like to find out as well." DS Carruthers stated.

DS Carruthers knew how he felt. She could not have children, she had tried with her husband on many occasions, but sadly failed. IVF treatment was out of the question, they couldn't cover the expense. Her and her husband felt cheated, but it was a turning point. DS Carruthers excelled as a PC and was promoted to the Luton CID where she eventually became a Detective Sergeant.. Her husband changed completely, he blamed her for not conceiving he became controlling and coercive and made her life hell.

"Is that why you were having endless affairs?" DC Dempster asked.

"Me and Sandra drifted apart, I fucked around and met woman on line.

When she found out she stopped having sex with me, so I continued, then I met Annabelle and I started to have a serious relationship. I love her and I want her in my life. I just feel guilty about Sandra being murdered, because I wasn't there to protect her. Like I said I loved her dearly, it was circumstances that change mine and Sandra's world."

"Johan I'm going to touch on something else! Please bear with me…According to Sandra's GP she was a chronic cocaine abuser. Her doctor tried to tell her that it was dangerous to her health. Did you know about that? DS Carruthers asked.

"Yeah, me and Mrs Sweeting tried to stop her, at one point we thought she given it up. But she started using again. She had been using most days. I think she had to blocked out all the hurt and pain, from her early life and the fact she couldn't conceive."

"Is that why you cheated on her?" DC Dempster asked.

"Yes, probably." Johan bowed his head in shame, "I suppose I let it carry on lately because I was in love with Annabelle."

"Maybe you can help us with the name of her dealer?" DS Carruthers asked.

"All I know she called him Ralphy; I don't know anything else. She was very sneaking with her using, but I knew she was. Do you think it was a drug deal gone wrong?"

"Let's us do the figuring out, Mr de Villiers?"

DS Carruthers snapped. Johan put his hands up in surrender.

"Oh yes, I found Sandra's old pay as you go mobile phone, I wondered if it would be any good to you?" DS Carruthers was excited this could be the key to the investigation.

"You should have told us earlier?" Where is it Mr de Villiers." DS Carruthers scathed.

"I didn't think. I found it in the Welsh dresser in the living room."

"What time do you get home?" DS Carruthers probed.

"Around 7pm, depending on the traffic on the A2580."

"I will send an officer to collect it." DS Carruthers snapped.

"I didn't kill her or arranged for someone to murder her. I loved her that's why I couldn't divorce her. She wouldn't last in the real world." Johan pleaded to his detriment.

DS Carruthers was angry about the mobile phone, but somewhere in her body she believed him.

"Well, thank you, there are no other questions?" They all shook hands and the detectives left him to his back-log of patients.

On the way back to the incident room DS Carruthers, called control and spoke to the desk Sergeant and explained that she needed something urgent collecting.

"Is PC Sanders on duty this evening?"

"Yes, he's just come on."

"Can you send him to this address it's the Old Granary, Trussington Village. Tell him to be there for 7pm because the resident Johan de Villiers is coming from work. Tell him to take latex gloves and an evidence bag with him and return the mobile phone to forensics."

"Ok, DS Carruthers."

CHAPTER SIXTEEN

The incident room was fairly quiet, everyone had their noses to the grindstone. It was nearly five pm. The DCI was pleased with their findings, but he felt they were going around in circles. DS Carruthers and DC Dempster wasn't going to leave for another 45 minutes for Grayson so they went for a break in the canteen.

Grayson was on the other side of the Halstead Estate. It was a leafy and affluent suburb compared to the rest of Stowgarth. The detectives arrived at the Grayson Community Centre. It was nearly 6pm. The car park was full. So, they parked on a narrow street opposite. As usual, a resident came and told them not to park there. The detectives showed their Police Warrants and the resident went back into his house with his tail firmly between his legs. The main hall was full of dogs of different types and sizes. They were all pedigree dogs; Chihuahuas, Terriers, Cockers, Golden Retrievers and Labradors and many more she couldn't not name.

The detectives looked for Samantha Mealing. DS Carruthers spoke to an old lady with red framed glasses who was holding a shivering pug puppy with shiny blue sparkly collar close to her chest. She pointed her in the right direction. Samantha Mealing was a small plump in her fifties. She had azure blue eyes and long mousy hair that was kept in a pony tail, it trailed down her back. She wore blue jeans and a pink floral blouse.

"Hello, are you Samanatha Mealing?"

"Yeah, that's me." Samantha Mealing spoke in a local accent.

"I'm DS Carruthers and this is DC Dempster."

"I was expecting you; I was a very close friend to Sandra. The news was shocking I'm surprised I'm here tonight. We all loved Sandra here and at the dog shows up and down the country. She will be sadly missed." Samantha tears prickled her eyelids and her voice thickened, "Shall we talk in the foyer it will be more private."

The foyer walls were plastered with leaflets advertising classes and events at the centre. They sat down on a soft cheap fabric sofa facing each other.

"How can I help you?" Samantha began. A tear rolled down her face, 'I didn't want to be here today, but Sandra would have told me off for not opening up."

"Have you and Sandra been running this ringcraft long?" DS Carruthers was courteous and let her speak. She could see she was finding it very difficult.

"About 5 years." Samantha took a tissue out her jeans pocket and dabbed her eyes.

"When did you last see Sandra?" and how did she seem?" DS Carruthers looked at DC Dempster to take over.

"On Saturday we went to the Cambridgeshire Championship Dog Show at Peterborough Showground. It was a good day all round, we both got placed with our dogs. Actually, she got two firsts with Norma and Cassidy. I breed and show English Pointers. Sandra was quiet and distant. To be honest she had not been herself for a while. I just assumed she was having problems with Johan again. We did not talk about it because she knew my feelings on the matter. I had told her on numerous occasions to leave him, but she never listened to me."

"Do you know of anybody who would want to murder Sandra?" DC Dempster asked. Samantha shook her head to the left then the right, "Did she have any enemies?"

"No, not Sandra."

"What about her car being damaged twice at dog shows?" DC Dempster probed.

"They were isolated incidents, just sheer jealousy. Sandra was not liked because she showed and groomed her Golden Retrievers to perfection. Winning was routine for Sandra and her dogs, and people didn't like it."

"Did you know she was pregnant?"

"Hell, no, she couldn't conceive. She didn't tell me everything she was a very closed book. Never really showed emotions. Probably living with that pig ignorant man, didn't help. He just gave up on here because she couldn't conceive.

"Do you know who could be the father?" DC Dempster added.

"Well, it won't be Johan de Villier. She wouldn't sleep with him under anaesthetic. I assure you."

"You seem very bitter about her husband?" DS Carruthers interrupted.

"He's ogre and that's why she died." Samantha was angered and very upset.

"Let's get on with my questioning, did you know she was a cocaine addict?" DS Carruthers probed further. There was an awkward silence.

"Not at first, I just thought it was her character. At times she became extremely alert and intensely happy, euphoric then other times she was as low as snakes' belly. Then I caught her snorting cocaine in the back of my car at a dog show. When I asked? She told me about Johan's many affairs and miscarriages etc. It was the thing only that deadened the pain and it helped her mood and she forgot about her worries for a while. From what I gathered she had been taking it awhile. I think she used it as a crutch to lean on."

"How did it affect your friendship?"

"Awkward at first, but she said she would stop, she realised it was affecting her health. I went on and on at her. I told I would support her. It had taken me years, but last week she agreed to come here to a drug abuse and recovery meeting. It went well. Then this happens." Samantha sobbed again.
"Did you know about her brother Daniel?" DS Carruthers continued.

"Yes, but she told me to keep it to myself."

"What did she tell you about him?"

"That he had only came into her life just recently. She told me about her childhood and her parents who were addicts, so it was no surprise that she had a sibling. I know she helped him off the streets, but she did not say anything else."

"You have given us some interesting insights to work on. Thank you for your help. If you think of anything else then please give me a ring at the station." DC Dempster handed her a card with Serious Crime Unit on it." Samantha gripped her arm as DS Carruthers was leaving.

"Please find the killer."

"We will." DS Carruthers was adamant. The detectives exited the building leaving Samantha and the barking dogs behind.

The detectives drove back to the police station. DC Dempster was surprised, she wasn't a cold fish as he first thought.

DC Dempster was singing to the song on the radio. afterwards the DJ Cody Scott read out the local news headlines: THE MURDER OF A LOCAL WOMAN SANDRA de VILLIERS. ENQUIRES ARE GOING ON-GOING AND TOMMOROW NIGHT THERE WILL BE A POLICE PRESS RELEASE....THERE AS BEEN ANOTHER ARMED ROBBERY IN STOWGARTH AT THE HAMMONDS BOOKMAKERS AT REDMILE SHOPPING PRECINCT. IT WAS APPROXIMATELY AT 6PM. ONE OF THE OWNERS WAS SHOT AT

THE SCENE AND IS IN HOSPITAL. NOBODY ELSE WAS INJURED. PLEASE IF YOU HAVE ANY INFORMATION ON THESE INVESTIGATION'S PLEASE GET IN TOUCH WITH ME OR STOWGARTH POLICE.

DS Carruthers knew that the DJ Cody Scott was known for revealing big news before it was released.

"It's been released and we don't know anything about it. I suppose DS Munro and her team are dealing with it. We have a major leak this is not the first time this has happened." DS Carruthers was annoyed.

When the detectives got to the incident room it was a cacophony of noise. Then they realised the extent of the armed robbery from DCI Barnes.

"Thank you, please you both have worked later than normal go home and I will see you in the morning."

"Thanks Guv." The detectives said in unison.
DS Carruthers went to get a taxi by the Stag Inn. She was going to go in but she had a very busy day. Then she heard a beep behind her. It was DC Kapoor in his spanking new car.

"Hey, do you want to go for a Chinese I've

been resting all day and feel much better now."

DS Carruthers told him about the questioning of Johan de Villiers and Samantha Mealing. She only told him what she knew about the armed robbery.

"Yes, I heard on the radio. Bloody Cody Scott. I would love him to get his comeuppance."

"Yeah, me too!"

"Have you met him before?" Faith asked.

"Yes, at a garden party he was all mouth no trousers." DC Kapoor smiled.

"Anyway, let's go." Vikram grabbed her and kissed her. Faith was overjoyed. She had forgotten how tired she felt.

It was 9.50pm. Cody Scott was coming out of the Radio Stowgarth FM buildings on mount street in the town centre. Cody's mobile phone buzzed in his coat pocket. He retrieved it the and read the message from Hugo Molinari. Cody was pleased he had taken his advice about renting the second floor of the warehouse. Cody walked to his brand new elegant red sports car. It was on the opposite side of the street. As he approached his car, someone jumped out from the shadows of a doorway that faced the convertible. He took Cody by surprise.

"Are you Cody Scott?" The man shouted.

"G'day mate, who's asking?"

The tall wiry lad who wore a black bandana on his head. He charged at Cody knocking him to the ground. The lad kicked and beat him. Cody's assistant was heading to her car, it was parked next to Cody's convertible. She looked in horror. The lad let go of Cody and ran off in the direction of the market place. Cody was on the ground covered in blood. Penny phoned the emergency services.

Two uniformed officers arrived at the crime scene of the assault then the ambulance appeared. Cody's assistant gave the male officer a description of the attacker and told him what she saw. He got in touch with police control and they put out a description to everyone on duty that night in and around Stowgarth to keep an eye out for the attacker. Cody was in severe pain, he was covered from head to toe in cuts and bruises. It looked like he had some broken bones. The paramedics instantly gave him pain relief then they put him on a stretcher and lifted him into the ambulance. Cody's assistant went to Lincoln County Hospital with him, the PC's followed them to the hospital. They needed to take the relevant statements.

SAME TIME. DIFFERENT PLACE.

The detectives were tucking into their Chinese food, they chose a tiny intimate place to sit in the restaurant. They ate under seductive lamp lighting. Faith had her favourite sweet and sour chicken. Vikram had vegetable chow mein. They shared a bowl of fluffy rice and prawn crackers. Faith had nearly drunk a whole bottle of sparkling white wine while Vikram was on his second bottle of Orangina.

"I thought you was giving me the cold shoulder?" Faith said.

"Don't be so silly." He reached for her hand, "I told you I'm sorry for disappearing this morning, you are just what I need at the moment...We said we did not want to have anything too complicated." Vikram squeezed her hand. Faith felt the chemistry and passion between them. She blushed, but he recognised the difference in her face.

"What about your impeding marriage to Chadda?"

"I've not got there yet, let's just see where this takes us? Vikram demanded. They mirrored each other's smile.

An hour or two later and another bottle of

wine supped, Faith was tipsy. They left the restaurant hand in hand. Ivy Street was only 20 minutes away. A fire engine roared pass them in all its glory. When they got to Faith's Street, they could see the fire brigade putting out a burning car. As they approached it was outside Faith's front door. Vikram realised that it was his brand new car had been deliberately set on fire. They kept their distance until it had been put out by the fire crew. A police car had arrived at the smoking wreck. The detectives were surprised to see the detectives. The fire brigade said it was safe for them to enter Faith's property. The uniformed officers started knocking on doors on the street to see if anybody saw or heard anything.

Faith had sobered up quickly, she made Vikram a black coffee and she opened a bottle of her favourite whiskey. A knock came at the door, Vikram answered.

"Here's your crime number mate, sorry nobody heard or saw anything. We will up our patrol of the area. Sorry, that's all we can do." The male uniformed officer said. Then he bobbed his head to the side, "Are you seeing the ICE QUEEN then?" He said it so Faith could hear it.

"FUCK OFF." Vikram slammed the door in his face. He went in the lounge and sat next to Faith. Vikram was devastated. He had only had the car a matter of weeks. It was his pride and joy. He wasn't sure if she heard what the male uniformed officer had said,

"So that's what they call me at the station?"

"Don't worry about it they are just being nobs."

"I find it quite amusing." Faith smiled.

Vikram poured himself whiskey.

"You don't drink VIKRAM KAPOOR."

"Well, I think this counts as a good exception." Vikram laughed. He drank it, he winced and coughed. Faith laughed.

"It's like drinking petrol." Vikram put his hands to his face.

"No, its fuel from the star ship enterprise." Faith laughed. She put an arm around him. Vikram was surprised by the show of affection. Faith was known as the ice queen, but she had definitely thawed towards him. They kissed and she took him and the drinks too bed.

CHAPTER SEVENTEEN
Tuesday 20th December 2016

The briefing was short and sweet this morning. Last night Ricky Hammond the bookmaker had died in hospital due to his injuries. So, it was now a man-hunt for the two-armed robbers. The DCI wanted to brief DS Munro's investigation team.

DS Carruthers went back to her desk, she inputted the name Daniel Hardy in the criminal records database. His mug-shot popped up on the screen. He looked like his sister's photo on the evidence board. They had the same facial profile and coloured hair. Daniel Hardy had a string of convictions; theft, burglary, drunk and disorderly and drug possession. His address at the time of the offences was 8 Coxmoor Close on the notorious Halstead Estate.

DS Carruthers grabbed DI Reads attention. He came over to her desk. He was pleased with her findings.

"When you have had your coffee you and you're DC can go and question him."

DS Carruthers grabbed another fresh coffee from the machine. DC Kapoor had come back from sick, but they both know they spent the night together again.

The detectives stood whispering. A phone rang continuously. Much to DCI Barnes displeasure,

"Can someone please answer that phone?"

DS Carruthers realised it was her phone. She sheepishly walked to her desk. She felt like everyone was watching her every move. DS Carruthers picked up the phone and took in the information. When she came off the phone, she gained DCI Barnes attention.

"Yes, DS Carruthers."

"That was Sergeant Ross. Stowgarth's minor celebrity DJ Cody Scott was beaten to a pulp last night outside the Radio station building. He is stable in hospital. He has cuts and bruises to his face, neck, torso and arms. Cody has a dislocated shoulder that needs an operation. He has a broken nose, and numerous fractured ribs. Someone wanted to teach him a lesson. I don't think this has anything to do with our current investigations, but I thought it was important enough to interrupt."

"Cody Scott does have a tendency to delve into matters he does not know anything about, but that does not mean he should be violently attacked.

Thank you, DS Carruthers, for bringing that to our attention." DCI Barnes smiled.

DC Kapoor found it hard to park the blue unmarked vehicle on the close. He managed to squeeze it between two brand new cars. Coxmoor Close was full of semi-detached brick town houses. Most of them was council properties, only a few were privately owned. Number 8 looked scruffy from the outside. The wooden front door needed painting urgently. The curtains in the white UPVC windows were very dirty and thread bare. The garden was no better; there was an old scrapheap on the drive. There was a rusty green car. It had no wheels, no doors, a smashed windscreen and a missing bonnet. The hedgerow was tall and overgrown. The detectives walked up the broken crazy paving slabs towards the front door.

"It's like Onslo and Daisy's house in that programme on BBC One." DC Kapoor said. They both laughed.

DS Carruthers rapped her knuckles on the wooden door. A woman answered, she was in her late 50s. She had a cigarette dangling from her mouth. She was large set with large pendulous breasts. She had shoulder length wavy bleached blond hair with terrible dark roots. She had pale blue eyes and matching lipstick. She wore blue holey jeans and a dirty yellow out-dated reebok sweater.

"Hello, can I help?" The lady said in a smoky voice.

The detectives showed their Police Warrants. She paused, turned and shouted.

"Billy, will you turn down that fucking television." Then she turned back to the detectives.

"I would let you come in, but my husband hates coppers and I don't want him in another bad mood." She paused to take a full lung of nicotine.

"Like I said, can I help?" The lady snapped.

"Are you Daniel Hardy's mum?" DS Carruthers asked.

"Yeah, I'm Sheila Hardy, what has that tow-rag done now."

"He has done nothing wrong; we just want to ask him some questions? Does he live here?" DC Kapoor asked.

"No, he's not lived here since he was 21."

"Do you have address for him?"

"He lives in the centre of Stowgarth 33 Newbold Street opposite the train station.

DS Carruthers wrote it down on his notepad. The detectives were pleased with their findings. They got back in the unmarked police car and drove towards the town centre.

DC Kapoor navigated the one-way system with ease. The High Street was teeming with buses and Christmas shoppers. They headed towards the train station. It was in a row of old stone terrace houses similar to Ivy Street. DS Carruthers let DC Kapoor take the lead on this one.

DC Kapoor rang the doorbell. A frail old man answered the door.

"Hello." He said in an inaudible voice. He was a small plump man with a reddened face. He wore dark brown trousers and a grey holey jumper and he stunk of gin. The detectives flashed their police warrants in his direction.

"Does Daniel Hardy live here?" DC Kapoor asked.

"Nope, I threw him out yonks ago. I caught him smoking cannabis in his room. I think at first, he slept on the streets and sofa surfed. Then I saw him up town. I am sure it was in early September. I had just come back from Blackpool from my daughters. He looked a changed lad. He was clean shaven and he had new clothes on. Daniel looked like he was off the drugs. He said he had moved into a terrace house on Balfour Street, New Marsh, Stowgarth. The detectives were pleased with the information.

The detectives went back to the unmarked police car. They had parked at the end of the street. DS Carruthers rang DC Booth at the Serious Crime Unit to find out if Daniel Hardy's address was on the council tax or electoral registers. It came back blank. DS Carruthers thought: *I wonder?*

"DC Booth, try the name Sandra de Villiers?" She searched the council databases.

"Bingo, it's number 14 Balfour Street." DC Booth announced.

"Perfect. Thanks DC Booth." DS Carruthers replied happily.

"Fine Police work, Detective Sergeant Carruthers." DC Kapoor mimicked. Det. Chief Super Hargreaves voice.

New Marsh was in the north east of Stowgarth. In its centre was a massive park and recreational ground. In August every year for five days it was home to a traveling fair. Balfour Street was facing the park's entrance. They parked nearby and briskly walked up to number 14. DS Carruthers rang the doorbell, she could hear the television coming from inside. Frustrated, DC Kapoor rang the doorbell again. A young man opened the door.

"Hello."

"Are you Daniel Hardy?" DS Carruthers asked.

"Yeah, that's me." The young man said.

Daniel Hardy was about 5foot7, terribly thin he needed a good meal down him. He had thick spiky ginger hair, pale blue eyes and freckles. He wore blue jeans and a black hoodie. Daniel Hardy was the spitting image of his sister. They both had high cheekbones.

"You have been very difficult to track down. I am DS Carruthers and this is DC Kapoor." They showed him their police warrants, "You're not in trouble."

Daniel Hardy showed them into a dark small lounge heavy dark curtains were still closed. The room was untidy and there was the stale smell of cannabis. There was a massive television on the chimney wall.
A man roughly the same age as Daniel Hardy was sitting on a brown material three-seater sofa.

He was an intense looking lad with unfortunately goofy teeth, he looked taller than Daniel Hardy. He had short brown hair with a forces parting. He had oval brown eyes and short well-kept beard. He was wearing grey jogging bottoms and an up-to-date Spanish home football shirt. DS Carruthers noticed he was full of tattoo's, he had a beautiful arum lily on his neck. The lads must have been playing on their play-station, an adventure game had been paused on the screen. The makeshift coffee table had loads of takeaway cartons, beer cans and bottles of cider.

"It's the Police!" Daniel Hardy announced. The lad on the sofa looked surprised by their appearance.

"Daniel, you better take a seat…We have some bad news." DS Carruthers always found this part of the job the hardest. "Your sister was found murdered on Friday evening at 5.10pm." DS Carruthers explained where she was found and the circumstances.

"I have only just found her." Daniel Hardy said shocked and clearly upset. Then he shouted with anger,

"This is her husband. She rang me crying on Thursday night and told me that her husband knew about me and he had prohibited her from seeing me."

"How did you take it?" DC Kapoor asked.

"I wasn't happy about it, but she said she would ring me next time her husband had gone to work. I waited and waited and then rang her and her phone was dead. So, I assumed I wouldn't see her again. I was angry, and I felt sorry for her living with a man like that."

"When was the last time you saw her?" DS Carruthers asked delicately.

"She used to come on a Tuesday night but she changed it to a Thursday about four weeks ago."

"Do you know why?"

"No, she loved our company but she hardly spoke about her life…we always order a couple of pizzas and watch the television. Sandra loved her soaps on television."

"How did she seem the last time you saw her?" DS Carruthers continued.

"To be honest the last couple of weeks she had not been herself…She was down in the dumps and she wasn't sleeping very well."

"Sandra was a cocaine addict, was you, her

supplier?" DC Kapoor interjected. Daniel Hardy was stunned, lost for words. DS Carruthers smiled inwardly. DC Kapoor got results, but he had a very laid-back attitude to policing.

"No, she always came with it and we shared it." The other man said openly.

"Do you know anybody who may want to hurt her?"

"I didn't know her long; my sister was a lovely woman?" Daniels eyes were full of tears.

"I have to ask where you both were on Friday evening at 5.10pm?"

"I was here with Richard. We watched a quiz on television then played on the play-station.." Daniel said. The man nodded.

"Can I have your full name Richard?" DC Kapoor asked.

"Richard Jeffrey Downing."

"Do you live here with Daniel Hardy?"

"Yes, we share the bills."

DC Kapoor took his statement about the

phone call on Thursday night.

"Thank you for your help, we will keep you informed how the investigation goes." DS Carruthers said, "We are sorry for your loss?"

"Ok, Thank you." Daniel said shutting the door behind them.

The detectives walked back to their unmarked police vehicle.

"Someone's had a good time." DS Carruthers announced.

"The bastards must have been watching us?" DC Kapoor moaned. Someone had keyed the unmarked police car.

"Well, they must have an eye for the law." DS Carruthers said.

They got in the car; DC Kapoor was furious.
"Why are you so upset." DS Carruthers laughed.

"It's a bloody mess." DC Kapoor scowled.

"It's not even your car. Just report it to Car Services. They will paint or polish the scratch's out."

"Yeah, I suppose so." DC Kapoor agreed. "What did you think of Daniel Hardy?"

"He seemed upset, but his alibi was a little feeble, but it will be hard to prove otherwise unless we have some clear evidence. I thought the other lad looked a bit shifty."

"Yeah, well dodgy." DC Kapoor agreed.

"But what was interesting is that Johan knew about Daniel and tried to stop Sandra seeing him. It's another lie from Mr de Villiers. We will have to question him again." DS Carruthers stated.

DC Kapoor put the car in gear and disappeared from the street.

CHAPTER EIGHTTEEN

The drive through was busier than normal,

"Wouldn't it be good if we could just put on blue lights and sirens on and every car moves out the way for us and we get to the front of queue." DC Kapoor Joked.

They both laughed.

DC Kapoor wasn't hungry, but DS Carruthers tucked into a hamburger and fries. They both sat drinking coffee while they listened to the radio.

"It seems strange that Cody Scott is not on the radio. I wonder how he is doing in the hospital. I know we said he should get his comeuppance, but we didn't want him to be violently assaulted." DS Carruthers said.

"It's a good job we were together at the Chinese restaurant." DC Kapoor smiled.

"What you going to do about your car?"

"I spoke to my insurance company first thing and they are delivering a courtesy car to the station. I have let Sergeant Ross know on reception."

"What are we doing Serg, are we going to see Johan de Villiers?"

"No, that can keep…we need to go back to the police station."

The Incident room was quiet, most of the unit had gone for their dinner in the station's canteen. DS Carruthers and DC Kapoor grabbed a coffee from the hot drinks machine and made their way over to their desks. DS Carruthers answered a few emails then she remembered to look up Richard Jeffrey Downing on the criminal records database. He had a long criminal record, all kinds of petty thieving, drug possession and drug dealing. DS Carruthers looked further into his file, five years ago he was caught giving a man a blow-job in a car on the Stowgarth Retail Park by a patrolling policeman. What was ironic was that the man was Cyril Snow, he was a judge at the local magistrate's court. They were both charged accordingly. The scandal was all over the papers. Mr Snow was made to resign from his position on the queen's bench.

DS Carruthers realised she had to also look up the name or surname Ralphy. She drew a blank. Suddenly a thought came to her: *"I should run it past the drug squad to see if anybody has heard of a dealer or abuser called Ralphy."* DS Carruthers grabbed herself another coffee and headed for the lift.

The lift door opened and she was surprised to see DCS Hargreaves. He was standing alone holding a bunch of box files. He had a big pervy smile on his face. He made DS Carruthers shudder. DCI Barnes told her he was retiring in the new year.

"Hello, Sir." DS Carruthers said politely.

"What floor do you require?"

"The top floor please, Sir."

DCS Hargreaves pressed the buttons for the acquired floors, the door closed and the lift started to ascend.

"How is the Sandra de Villiers case going." DS Carruthers thought: *"I do not know why he is asking me. He gets a daily update by DCI Barnes."*

"We are getting there. I'm on my way up to the drug squad just following up a potential lead." There was a moments uneasy silence then the doors opened on to the third floor.

"Goodbye Detective Sergeant Carruthers, keep up the good work." He stepped out the lift. A whiff of strong cologne lingered behind. The doors closed again and the lift ascended upwards.

The drugs unit was eerie quiet, there was nobody in sight. Then a voice stopped her in her tracks. He was tall, athletic and he oozed sheer sexual magnetism. He had a shaven head and oriental features. DS Carruthers noticed straight away he was wearing gold wedding band. That was a let-down, but at least he was easy on the eye.

"Can I help?"

"Yes, I'm from SCU?" The detectives introduced themselves. DS Carruthers pushed her fringe out of her face and pouted her lips. She really wanted to have Botox, but she was afraid of needles. She only went to the dentist when she was only in agony with her teeth.

"Where is everyone?" DS Carruthers asked.
"It's this mystery bug. I am the only senior officer on duty today. The rest of the depleted team have gone paintballing on a unit bonding session. Over the last few month's, we have had an intake of new faces. So, I have been answering the phone and doing boring paperwork.

"Sorry, why do I have the pleasure of your company?" the officer smiled; his shiny teeth were all veneers. She wondered if it the work had been done by Johan de Villiers. DS Carruthers explained the present murder case she was on.

"The victim was a cocaine addict and we found out that her dealer was named Ralphy? Does that name or surname ring a bell? I have run it through the normal channels, but I drew a blank."

"I've never heard that name. I have only been here around six months, but I will ask around the unit. Somebody is bound to know, or have come across the name."

"Thanks. I look forward to your findings?"

"It's been nice seeing you." DS Robson said.

"It's nice to be seen." DS Carruthers replied. She turned and walked away. The lift was busy so she decided to take the staircase down to the Incident room.

DS Carruthers needed a caffeine boost so she had a double expresso from the hot drinks machine. She carried it over to her desk and sat down.

"Where have you been?" DI Read asked. He tapped her on her shoulder making DS Carruthers jump out of her skin.

"The drug squad, DI Read, Why?" Have I done something wrong?"

"Well, not really…Me, DI Love and DCI

Barnes have been looking at the investigation so far. We have over looked something? It's an error and it needs to be done this afternoon." DI Read stated. DS Carruthers looked perplexed.

"What have we over looked?"

"She worked at the dance school; we haven't had a statement from her employer."

"Ok, me and DC Kapoor will go there now."

"Thanks, DCI Barnes will be pleased."

The dance school was in a huge warehouse building on Cavendish Road in Grayson. It was once a well-known hosiery factory. The wooden reception desk was striped back and lightly varnished. Nobody was stationed there. The walls were painted brightly in magnolia with black stencilled dancers in different poses. There were two large black leather chesterfields. There was a dancing class taking place behind two glass and chrome doors. They assumed the man teaching was the owner. The detectives took a seat. DC Kapoor looked at his mobile phone, it was fast approaching 3pm.

Suddenly a group of nimble octogenarians appeared from the dance studio. There was one old man and about nine old women. The dance instructor followed behind them with a mobile stuck to his ear. The detectives stood-up. They flashed their police warrants in his direction.

"I'm just taking this important call, I will not be long, grab yourself a coffee from the hot drinks machine behind the reception desk." He rushed into his office slamming the door behind him.

CHAPTER NINETEEN

Ten minutes later an annoyed Hugo Molinari came off his mobile phone. He appeared red faced and flustered.

"I'm sorry about that but my ex-wife is trying to bleed me dry." He screamed dramatically. "Do you want to come through to my office?"

The office was fairly big. Hugo Molinari dark wooden desk and swivel brown leather chair was in front of a full-length window that looked on to the dance studio. There were two large metal filing cabinets on top was a white wireless printer. Hugo Molinari laptop was nowhere to be seen, probably tucked away in a drawer somewhere. A large black 65inch flatscreen television was mounted on the wall. There was a large wooden shelving rack full of trophies, awards, and photos in matching gold-coloured frames.

"How can I help?" Hugo Molinari spoke with an Anglo-Italian accent. The detectives could see he was an intelligent man.

Hugo Molinari was born in Genoa in Italy. He was born a twin on the 23rd March in 1982 and he was presently 34 years old. He moved to Stowgarth, Lincolnshire, England in 1990 aged 8 with his mum, dad and sister. He went with Adriana to a local primary school then he went on to catering college in St Enochs. He was fantastic chef, but his passion was dancing. He opened his first Italian restaurant in St Enochs in 2006. It thrived and became a very profitable business. His mum and dad died a year apart; they left him and his sister a large inheritance. So, he opened two more restaurants. The Molinari Dance School was left to him, as Adrina no longer danced anymore. It was now a recognised dance school in Lincolnshire.

The detectives introduced themselves. DS Carruthers decided before entering the room that DC Kapoor was going to be doing the questioning.

"Is this about Sandra de Villiers? I wondered when you were going to appear?" Hugo Molinari said smugly.

"Yes, it is, how long has she worked here?" DC Kapoor began.

"She worked here for the last five years, on Wednesday and Thursday evenings. She worked from 5pm-9pm on both days. She taught ballroom and Latin dancing to a wide range of children with different capabilities. Then on Wednesday and Thursday evenings between 8pm until 9pm. She taught a group of adult's salsa dancing. She was a fantastic dancer and teacher. She loved teaching and her pupils loved her too. Sandra was a lovely woman, a bit complicated at times. But we were good friends. She will be terribly missed."

"May I ask what did you mean by she was a bit complicated at times?" DC Kapoor repeated the words, word by word.

"Sandra didn't have to come to work. Sandra had the life of a princess; her husband showered her with money. The problem was she was in a loveless marriage, her husband cheated on her all the time. Sometimes she would come to work in a right state and I was always a shoulder to cry on."

DS Carruthers took down some notes.

"Did you like to be her shoulder to cry on?" DC Kapoor asked.

"I was a good friend and colleague."

"So, you never had a sexual relationship with Sandra?" DS Carruthers jumped straight in going straight for the jugular.

"Like I said, I was a friend. We kept it professional at all times?" Hugo Molinari insisted.

"When did you last see Sandra de Villiers?" DC Kapoor continued.

"Here on Thursday evening usual time."

"Now, I find that very hard to believe Mr Molinari. We have a statement to say she was with someone else on Thursday night?" The blood drained from Hugo Molinari's face.

"Oh, well…." There was a long pause, "We had a falling out four weeks ago…don't know if I should say this but I found her sniffy coke in the cloakroom. I was mad so I told her to leave. She begged me not to say anything to her husband. I said I would pick up the slack while she got her head together and she agreed.

"When was the last time you saw her? And how was she?"

"About two weeks ago, she said she was looking into a drug addiction group. I said if she attended it regularly I would have her back here after the New Year…She was embarrassed about her drug addiction, but she seemed to be in a jovial mood and couldn't wait to come back to work."

"Do you know of any reason why someone would murder her?"

"No, definitely not…unless her husband had bumped her off." Hugo Molinari laughed. The detectives did not find it funny.

"Mr Molinari!!! this is a murder investigation it's not a joking matter, can you please answer my colleague's questions accordingly." DS Carruthers snapped.

"Where were you on Friday between 4pm and 6pm?" DC Kapoor continued.

"I don't work on Friday's. I was upstairs in my apartment with my twin boys. It's still a work in progress because it's being renovated and refurbished. Luckily the pool table is easily accessible so we played pool. We watched television and I ordered two pizzas. We ate them, the boys went to play on their play station and I watched a quiz show on BBC Two with a glass of red wine."

"Did you say you ordered a pizza?" DC Kapoor enquired, "What did you have? And where did you get it from?"

"I phoned pizzarama in Grayson around 4.00pm and it was delivered around 4.20pm. We had a Hawaiian and a pepperoni pizza, garlic bread with cheese and a bottle of diet coke."

DS Carruthers signalled to DC Kapoor that was enough of the questioning for now.

"Thank you, Mr Molinari, you have been

very helpful." DS Carruthers announced. She gave Hugo Molinari a card with the Serious Crime Unit on. The detectives exited the warehouse building.

"Something does not sit right with me. With all your experience, what did you think?" DC Kapoor asked.

"I thought he was a bit up his own arse, but that does not mean he murdered Sandra de Villiers. Good thinking about asking about where the pizza came from you can look into it when we get back to the station."

They were about to get into the unmarked police car.

"We have a problem; can you ring the garage and arrange transport for us."

"Why, what's the matter?" DC Kapoor was perplexed.

Two of the tyres were flat, with closer inspection they had been slashed.

"Twice in one day the garage aren't going to be pleased with us…and this is supposed to be a better place to live in Stowgarth." DC Kapoor sighed.

DC Kapoor rang the station to let them know what had happened. They arranged for the detectives to be picked up and the tyres to be changed.

The Incident Room was pretty quiet. Everyone was working at their desks writing up statements, answering emails and making phone calls. DS Carruthers spoke with DCI Barnes and told him their findings at Hugo Molinari's dance school.

DC Kapoor was determined to find out if Hugo Molinari's pizza alibi was true. DC Kapoor was normally steadfast, but he had the bit firmly between his teeth.

DS Carruthers brought two coffee's over to DC Kapoor desk. He had just come off the phone.

"That was the manager of pizzarama in Grayson. Hugo Molinari ordered the pizzas at 4pm and it was delivered twenty minutes later. The owner remembers Hugo calling because the shop had just opened and his was the first order.

"Don't get too disheartened we knew it was a long shot. You were brilliant questioning Hugo Molinari. Like I said to DCI Barnes, if the murderer is Hugo Molinari, then he will slip-up and we will be there to catch him. I've just ran his name through the criminal record database and he is clean as a whistle." DS Carruthers smiled, "and the sergeant on reception said your courtesy car has arrived and he has your car keys."

"Great, I wonder what they have sent me." DC Kapoor rubbed his hands with excitement.

The day had come to an end, both investigations had drew another series of blanks. DS Carruthers was being taken home by DC Kapoor, he got the keys and marched outside to the staff car park. Then his excitement turned sour. The courtesy car was a green four door saloon.

"Bloody hell, I've got to drive that heap of junk?" DC Kapoor pointed and moaned.

"It's a brand-new car, it's nice and shiny and the interior is excellent." You could see DS Carruthers didn't know anything about cars.

"It's from a car dealer you would of thought they send me a similar car to mine."

DC Kapoor moaned all the way back to DS Carruthers home on Ivy Street.

DC Kapoor was still pissed off. He didn't go inside, he kissed DS Carruthers on the cheek then drove off. DS Carruthers was glad he didn't come in because she wanted a long soak in the bath, before eating her chicken casserole that she had cooked in her slow cooker. DS Carruthers had half a bottle of red wine to finish off and she was going to watch her favourite soaps.

CHAPTER TWENTY
Wednesday 21st December 2016

DS Carruthers and DC Kapoor entered the Incident Room, they were jeered by the detectives who gathered for the morning's briefing.

"Who's getting married in the morning." DC Windass sang at the top of his voice.

"Grow up, you lot?" DS Carruthers scowled. The detectives gathered it had been spread around the station by the uniformed officers who attended DC Kapoor's car fire on Ivy Street. DS Carruthers and DC Kapoor just laughed it off. They hung up their winter coats and took a seat with the others. DC Windass blew kisses at DC Kapoor while the others laughed.

DI Love and DI Read did the morning briefing, DCI Barnes had phoned in sick with the mystery bug. DI Love was not long winded like his boss and kept it concise, but to the point.

DS Carruthers went straight to her desk. She looked up Johan de Villiers contact mobile number and gave him a ring.

"Hello is that Mr de Villiers?"

"Yes."

"It's DS Carruthers, we need to question you again. When will you be free to see us?"

"I'm at home. I'm off this morning, I'm going into work this afternoon."

"I will be with you within the next hour." DS Carruthers stated.

"I look forward to it." Johan said with sarcasm.

DS Carruthers and DC Kapoor arrived in Trussington Village.

"I meant to ask you, how was your day working with DC Dempster?" DC Kapoor asked.

"I thought him and DC Windass were clowns to be honest, but he surprised me. Did you know he has a degree in History and Archaeology? He told me about the history of St Francis Church here in Trussington. He is a very intelligent individual. I actually enjoyed working with him. I saw him in a completely different light."

"I think he as a girlfriend at the moment." DC Kapoor laughed.

"Not like that dickhead, he has the making of being a very good detective."

The roads were packed with traffic, it was the village Christmas market. Cars were parked on both sides of the road. DS Carruthers drove the blue Unmarked police car at a snail's pace, they eventually made it onto Kiln Lane.

Johan de Villiers Audi TT, a metallic Pink Kia Picanto and a brand-new gold two door sports car were on the drive.

DS Carruthers rang the bell, a young woman answered the door. DC Kapoor eyes instantly popped out his head and he was drooling at the mouth. The detectives realised straight away that the young woman was Annabelle Wolfe.

Annabelle was about 5foot6, she looked like a tanned barbie doll. She wore a cream polo high neck long sleeve cable knitted jumper dress. It did not leave much to the imagination. The young woman, was in early twenties, she had long straight blond hair and sparkling blue eyes. Her lips were enhanced and her teeth were polished white veneers. The detectives flashed their police warrants in her direction.

"Good morning, I'm DS Carruthers and this is DC Kapoor. Can we come in?"

"Yes, we have been expecting you." Annabelle let them into the hallway and closed the door behind them.

Annabelle showed them into the lounge. Johan was sat watching a chat show on the television. He was wearing grey cargo pants and a green and yellow Springboks Rugby Union Shirt.

"Good morning, Mr de Villiers. I saw another car outside is Mrs Sweeting here?" DS Carruthers asked.

"Yes, she is in the kitchen…Annabelle I'm going to have to ask someone to collect you and take you to the police station, we need to ask you some questions. Those questions will be taped."

DC Kapoor phoned the police station, luckily there was a patrol car in the area. Someone will be here in ten to fifteen minutes.

"Now Annabelle has gone I will ask you some questions in here while DC Kapoor will ask Mrs Sweeting some questions in the kitchen.

Johan sat in the wooden rocking chair.. He had not long come back from the gym, he smelled sweaty and he was red-faced.

"This is the third time we have had to

question you? Why didn't you tell us who Daniel was? You knew who he was and his relationship to your wife?"

Johan sat like a petulant child with his arms crossed in defiance. He just stared in the direction of the detectives.

"Come on Johan, I would like an explanation?" DS Carruthers snapped.

"We had an argument. I went through her personal things and found her bank statements. I was fed up with her spending my hard-earned money like it was going out of fashion. She had a tenancy for a three bedroomed house on Balfour Street in New Marsh. I knew she was keeping something from me. She made and answered calls privately in here. I asked her if she was having an affair, she broke down and she eventually told me about her brother. I was fuming with her, she was renting a house for him, spending my money on him. I told her to end the tenancy and stop seeing him. If she didn't, I would stop giving her allowance. I didn't tell you, because I felt it had nothing to do with the murder investigation."

"But you lied to us again? If you had told us earlier it would have saved us a lot of work."

"I'm sorry I will be totally transparent in the

future."

"Ok. If you lie to us again, we will have to take you down the station." DS Carruthers knew this was part of detective work, but she thought she would scare him.

DC Kapoor was in the kitchen. Mrs Sweeting was doing a high pile of washing.

"Good morning, Mrs sweeting, is it ok to ask you some more questions?"

"Yes, if I can continue with the ironing? I've got loads to be getting on with"

"Yes, that's fine." DC Kapoor agreed. He opened his notebook.

"Do you lie Mrs Sweeting?" DC Kapoor began. He didn't beat around the bush.

"No, I'm a Christian, you know I go to church, Why?" Mrs Sweeting said annoyed.

"Well, you like to fabricate and paper over the cracks and protect Johan de Villiers…You didn't tell us about his relationship with Annabelle Wolfe. You said all marriages had their difficulties, but you didn't tell us they hardly spoke and lived virtually separate lives…and you didn't even tell us about Johans philandering ways."

"I just didn't think it needed to be said." Mrs Sweeting said smugly.

"We are police detectives we always expect the truth, it is an on-going murder investigation." DC Kapoor stated, "You also did not tell us about Sandra cocaine abuse, is there anything else we should know? Did you know that Sandra's brother had found her and she was spending time with him."

"No, she never said, until Johan told me at the weekend."

"How did he take the news about Daniel?" DC Kapoor asked.

"Sandra had lied for months, of course he was angry. Johan was still protective over his wife, but he felt she had betrayed him."

"You also didn't tell us about Sandra's cocaine abuse? Did you ever see Sandra take it?"

"No, but I knew when she had taken it. She would turn the music up in the conservatory and dance for hours. Johan didn't like her taking it, ok she had highs, but when she didn't take it, she had terrible lows. He didn't like her taking it outside the house. He didn't like her driving around under the influence…We begged her to stop, but she wouldn't listen."

"Ok, well thank you for being honest this time." DC Kapoor finished his questioning and went back in the lounge.

"Well thank you Mr de Villiers. We will go and question Annabelle Wolfe now." DS Curruthers directed.

"Be gentle with her please. She can be very shy." Johan replied.

"She will be in safe hands." DS Carruthers laughed.

Annabelle was sat at the table next to her solicitor Mr Jason Raab.

She looked petrified, but DS Carruthers told her that she was not in trouble.

DC Kapoor turned on the digital recorder and DS Carruthers confirmed the date, time and place and the person's gathered around the table.

"Where is your accent from?" DS Carruthers enquired.

"I'm an East Sussex girl. I was born on the

south coast in Saltdean 4.7 miles from Brighton. I moved up here when I was eleven. My mum and dad are in the RAF. They are based at RAF Cranwell near the town of Sleaford." Annabelle said. She had calmed down now and seemed more relaxed.

"Can I ask where were you between 4pm and 6pm on Friday 16th December 2016?"

"I was at home in St Enochs with Johan. He arrived after 4pm. We watched television, had something to eat then we made love…then he went home."

"I know that Johan and Sandra had a strained marriage, but, but he wanted to stay married to his wife. Did this bother you in anyway?"

"Course it did, I love Johan, but no I didn't want her dead."

DS Carruthers finished the questioning. Annabelle and her solicitor were escorted out of the building. DS Carruthers and DC Kapoor were not surprised that Johan was telling the truth about him and his scarlet woman.

DS Carruthers that night had a really bad night, she had diarrhoea and she couldn't stop vomiting. She felt that bad that the following morning she phoned in sick. This was the first time in years she had to take time off work, but she felt lousy. She spent the whole day in bed. At tea time she felt really hungry so she had chicken soup and toast and luckily, she kept it down. DS Carruthers made herself an Irish coffee, she over did the whiskey as usual. She went into the lounge and watched her favourite soaps, by 10pm she was back in bed and she was now looking forward to the following day back at work.

CHAPTER TWENTY-ONE
Friday 23nd December 2016

DC Kapoor arrived at Ivy Street earlier than normal. DS Carruthers had texted him late last night to say she was feeling much better and could he pick her up a little earlier in the morning to take her to work. The snow had vacated Stowgarth and it had been replaced by heavy rain. In the distance he could hear a rumble of thunder and the odd strike of lightning. DS Carruthers was pleased to see him, she was heating up a pan of porridge oats and she was toasting two rounds of brown toast. She spread them lavishly with butter and marmalade. They sat eating their breakfast in the dining room.

The roads around Stowgarth Town Centre were flooding the rain was heavy and the drains could not cope with the deluge of water. The courtesy car windscreen wipers were not fast enough and the windscreen kept on steaming up to DC Kapoor's displeasure.

They got to the Incident room just in the nick of time. DCI Barnes had still not come in and now DC Windass had phoned in sick. DI Love took the briefing,

"If you are wondering, DCI Barnes will be on duty this afternoon…Well, we have some new developments…Sandra's pay as you go mobile phone has come back from forensics and Sandra was being blackmailed. We tried the blackmailer's phone, but it's dead. We checked the mobile phone number that called her on the night of her murder and it's the same number. So, the person who was blackmailing her lured her outside and murdered her." DI Love concluded.

DS Carruthers and her depleted investigation team went to their desks.

She was answering her emails when she spotted an email from DS Robson. He had found out who Ralphy was and needed her to ring him.

"Hello DS Robson, It's DS Carruthers."

"Hi DS Carruthers, sorry about the cloak and dagger email. I just felt I needed to speak to you personally over the phone with my findings."

"I have some good news for you. I have put my feelers out. Ralphy is actually Denise Dale. She is a known drug dealer. She has been convicted of drug possession and dealing many times before. According to sources she has gone to ground. She might have even moved away. I can give you her last known address, 102 Mulberry Court, Redmile. That's all the details I have."

"Thanks DS Robson. I will bring her up on the criminal records database. Then we will go and see what she has to say."

"DS Carruthers, I will be in the Stag Inn from 5.30pm…I can buy you a drink." DS Robson replied, "If I don't see you have a good Christmas."

"Yes, you too DS Robson."

DS Carruthers had put down the phone, she automatically regretted giving DS Robson the cold shoulder, he was handsome, suave and sophisticated. And she knew he would be great beneath the sheets, but she was developing feelings for DC Kapoor.

DS Carruthers browsed through the criminal records database. Denise Dale photofit flashed up on the screen of her laptop. She was much older than expected, she was in her early fifties. She was Afro-Caribbean, she had tight black curly hair and long eyelashes. She ran off a copy of photofit on her printer.

DS Carruthers went to see DI Love, she briefed him what she had found out.

"You and DC Kapoor might as well go this morning and find this Denise Dale…Don't forget you and DC Kapoor need to bring in your secret

Santa for the Christmas Party this evening."

"Don't worry about it DI Love we already put ours in the Santas sack."

"Good." DI Love smiled, and DS Carruthers went back to her desk.

The one-way system was bumper to bumper. It was lashing down with rain against the car windscreen. The deluge of water had caused chaos and mayhem. Some of the shops on the High Street were mopping up and sand bags were being placed in doorways. Nobody was aware of the incoming storm.

Once they got onto the main Redmile Road the traffic and the rain eased. Suddenly three concrete high-rise blocks of flats appeared before them. In the 80s and 90s Redmile had a bad name, but with local police working in the community the Estate had become a much safer and nicer area to live.

"Which one is Mulberry Court?" DS Carruthers asked.

"I think it's this one?" DC Kapoor pointed, "Yes, that's it."

The car park was chocka, they parked the car

in the emergency service bay. They emerged from the unmarked police car. A young guy with a shocking pink Mohican, numerous facial piercings and dressed in motorbike leathers opened the reception door for them. The detectives made their way to the lifts.

The lift opened onto the tenth floor. The smell of strong disinfectant hit their noses. DS Carruthers banged on the yellow wooden door of flat 102. The hallway light came on and the door opened a jar.

"Hello?" A timid voice came from within. The detectives showed her their police warrants. A lady opened the door fully. DS Carruthers was not sure if it was Denise Dale. The woman had a bald head, she had no eyelashes. She had sallow cheeks and sunken eyes.

"Are you Denise Dale?" DS Carruthers asked.

"Yes, you better come in?" Denise Dale replied.

The hallway was laminated wooden flooring and it had just been moped. The walls were painted yellow and they were emblazoned with family framed photographs. She showed them into the lounge area. It was clean and tidy. She must have been practicing Buddhism there was a shrine to Sakyamuni Buddha. The walls were decorated with buddhas on lotus flowers, pergolas and wheel of the life.

The detectives are asked to take a seat on the cream leather couch. Denise Dale sat in the chair opposite.

"How can I help?" Denise Dale replied with not much enthusiasm and energy.

"Do you know of a woman called Sandra de Villiers?" DS Carruthers showed her a photograph of her. Denise Dale did not say anything. She did not deny knowing her but she said she had a lot of customers.

"I gave up dealing 12 months ago. I have been on chemotherapy since the beginning of the year. I have terminal bowel and colon cancer."

"Oh, I'm sorry to hear that." DS Carruthers lied. She had no empathy for this woman she had been a dealer for years and spent time behind bars. She had wrecked a lot of people lives who was addicted to the drugs she sold. DS Carruthers knew it was crazy question but she had to ask,

"Where were on Friday 16th December between 4pm and 6pm?"

"I was in Lincoln Hospital. I had an operation last week. They took part of my colon away, but the cancer is too widespread. I only came out yesterday."

"Have you got the hospital and ward telephone number? We just need to follow it up?" DC Kapoor asked. Denise Dale looked inside her wooden sideboard. She handed a piece of paper to the detectives.

"You can take it with you." She mumbled.

"Do you know of anybody who could be her dealer?"

"No…There are hundreds of people she could have gone to in Lincolnshire."

The detectives thanked her and left the flat. They headed for the lifts.

The detectives walked back into the Incident room. They went to see DI Love, but he had gone to the canteen for a late breakfast. So, they went to their desks. DS Carruth1ers internal phone rang,

"Hello. DS Carruthers."

"I have a lady down here in reception that wants to speak to you about the Sandra de Villiers murder investigation." The duty Sergeant said.

"Thanks, we will come and speak to her."

DS Carruthers and DC Kapoor went down to reception. There were a handful of people, but there was only one woman.

"Are you here about the Sandra de Villiers murder investigation?"

"Yes." The woman replied.

"Come this way." DS Carruthers directed. She took her to a private room in the custody suite. They sat at a wooden table. DC Kapoor took notes and DS Carruthers asked questions where necessary.

"I'm DS Carruthers and this is DC Kapoor."

"I'm Sylvia Harris." She was in her early fifties and she had an hourglass figure. She had long blond curly hair and deep ocean blue eyes. She wore a black puffer jacket underneath was a top brand black trouser suit and stilettos. She wore hoodles of gold jewellery.

"I work in Manchester, Lancashire. I'm a Consultant at the Manchester Royal Infirmary."

"What field do you work in?" DC Kapoor asked.

"Medical...I work on accident and emergency. The hours are long, but I enjoy the challenge." Sylvia Harris said proudly.

"What can you tell us?" DS Carruthers was a little impatient. This could be the key to the investigation.

"I picked up your leaflet off the floor when I arrived home...I came home around 4pm on the 16th December 2016. I parked on the driveway as usual. I was in my lounge. It has a massive bay window that looks onto Gorton Road. At about 4.45pm a blue people carrier pulled up at the bottom of my drive. The problem on my road is that everyone parks where anybody wants too and there are always arguments. I went to ask him to move because I couldn't get out my driveway. I was going out later that night. As I got to the bottom of the driveway a man got out of the driver's seat of the car. I asked him to move, but he said he would not be long. I thought he was going to one of the surrounding houses, but he walked down the road towards Church Street. I was pissed off and I was going to wait for him to return, but it was a freezing night so I went back inside. About 5.15pm he returned to his car. He was all over the place, he seemed preoccupied he nearly got run over by a passing vehicle. He looked up at me in my bay window. He stuck two fingers up at me and hurriedly got in his car. Surprisingly he did a complete U-turn in the snow then sped-off towards the roundabout then right onto Edenfield Road.

"Can you describe this person for me?" DS Carruthers asked.

"I never took much attention to what he looked like. He was definitely younger than me. He was tall and slender. He wore a long dark trench coat and a black beanie hat. Oh, and he wore ski glasses."

"What kind of car was he driving?"

"I don't really know my cars." Sylvia Harris paused, "I went away for the weekend to my sisters in Macclesfield, Cheshire then I travelled to work from there on Monday. Luckily, I have now broken-up for Christmas. I came home this morning. So, instead of ringing you I thought I would pop in and see you. I was waiting a while in reception, because you were out. I'm glad I've seen you in person."

"Well, thank you." DS Carruthers said. DC Kapoor took Sylvia Harris's statement before he escorted Sylvia Harris out of the building while DS Carruthers went back to the Incident room.

CHAPTER TWENTY-TWO

DS Carruthers and DC Kapoor was stood at the coffee machine. The drinks came out lukewarm, somebody had accidentally knocked the switch off on the wall. So, they waited for the water to warm-up. The detectives stood talking.

DI Love came to speak with them.

"DS Carruthers, was your journey fruitful?" He asked.

"Well, DI Love, Denise Dale is terminally ill and very poorly. She was in hospital the day of Sandra de Villiers murder. She gave us a letter with the hospital details on it, DC Booth has followed it up and its kosher." DS Carruthers then told him about Sylvia Harris and the possible sighting of the killer.

"Things are warming up; I can feel it." DI Love said with optimism. He rubbed his hands and smiled.

It was 2pm. Everything had gathered in the Serious Crime Unit. DCI Barnes wanted to say a few things before the festivities began. He suspended the present investigations until after Christmas. He thanked everyone for their hard work over the last year.

"We are now breaking up for Christmas, but one person will not be coming back. Today is DI Love's last day as he is taking early retirement." Everyone jeered and applauded.

"DI Love, you will be sadly missed, your quick wit, your sheer tenacity and conscientious work ethic. DI Love, you're a fine detective, one of the best I have worked with. HAPPY RETIREMENT." The room erupted with cheers. DI Love stood up doing a Mexican wave in appreciation.

"I'm not worthy, I'm not worthy." He chanted. Everyone laughed, "Thank you for all your cards and presents and I am hoping to see you all tomorrow night at my retirement party. It's at my local public house, the Cross Keys in Sandwell. I hope you will give my predecessor an easy time. I am sure DI Read will make a fantastic replacement. If I don't see you tomorrow evening, it's been lovely working with you all and have a great Christmas."

"TO DI LOVE AND HAVE A GREAT RETIREMENT." DCI Barnes shouted. Every cheered and clapped.

"NOW, LETS GET ON WITH OUR CHRISTMAS STAFF PARTY." DI Love shouted at the top of his voice. Everyone cheered again.

DC Booth was in charge of the music. It was pumping loudly from a small Bluetooth stereo. Everyone helped themselves to the alcoholic drinks. There were assorted sandwiches and a mountain of mince pies they had all been prepared and baked by DCI Barnes wife. Everyone loved them. DC Booth handed around the charity pot.

"Come on everyone. Dig deep. Put your loose change in here." DC Booth demanded.

"DS Munro!" DCI Barnes shouted.

"Yes, Guv."

"Put a ten-pound note in the pot for all the times you have been late this year." DCI Barnes laughed.

"Yes, Guv." DS Munro moaned.

"One final push. I am going to total up soon." Alice disappeared to her desk.

Moments later she appeared with a beaming smile on her face. She announced that they had raised £375 pounds for their chosen charity the Stowgarth Homeless Shelter. They all cheered.

Everyone sat laughing, joking, drinking and

eating there was even a bit of dad dancing. The celebration was not rocking, but lively enough. Everyone was looking forward to the festive period and the welcomed break.

Secret Santa wrapped presents were individually chosen from the Christmas tubs. The girls had brought the boys presents and vice versa. DS Carruthers was not expecting much, but she got a lovely bottle of perfume. She had never heard of the brand, but it smelled beautiful. DS Carruthers had brought a men's grooming set from boots for an unknown male. She looked around the room, she was pleased that it had gone to DCI Barnes. He seemed happy with his present. The celebration fizzled out at 6pm. Everyone got their coats and disappeared. The younger detectives headed into town for more drinks. DS Carruthers and DC Kapoor were the last detectives to leave the unit. DCI Barnes and DI Love were standing talking near the exit to the stairwell.

"Merry Christmas." DS Carruthers kissed the senior detectives on their cheeks and DC Kapoor shook their hands.

"Merry Christmas you too." They said in unison.

DS Carruthers suggested they had a quick drink in the Stag Inn, she really wanted to see if DS

Robson had made it there, has he said he would. The rain had stopped. Stowgarth had a month's rainfall in one day. The road that the police station was still wet, but not flooded like earlier.

The Stag Inn was rammed with off duty police officers.

"Can I buy you both a drink?" DS Carruthers turned around to see PC Sanders stood next to the fruit machine.

"Yes please, I will have a vodka lime and lemonade and DC Kapoor will have a fresh orange and lemonade."

"Thank you." The detectives smiled.

DS Carruthers turned to look around the bar and saw DS Robson sat alone in one of the alcoves on the back wall. DS Robson looked hot and debonair. He was wearing a black striped three-piece suit; white shirt and he was not wearing a tie.

The detectives thanked PC Sanders and walked towards him; her heart was in her mouth.

"Hello, DS Carruthers and this is?" DS Robson held out his hand.

"I'm DC Kapoor."

"This is DS Robson, he helped us find Denise Dale."

DC Kapoor shook his hand. DS Carruthers sat down hesitantly beside him. He smelled hot and sexy.

"Did you find Denise Dale?" DS Robson asked. His eyes glistened in the overhead lights.

"Yeah, my assumption was that she was definitely her dealer some time ago. She looked shocking, she is dying of terminal cancer. DC Booth followed it up on the phone and it's the truth. We have crossed her off our list of possible suspects. Thank you for all your help." DS Carruthers concluded. They all sat talking for about 20 minutes or so.

DC Kapoor went to the toilet, leaving the other two alone.

"I really find you attractive." DS Robson said.

"Yes, your very attractive too, but we are both married." DS Carruthers said.

"Do you mean you prefer young puppies like DC Kapoor?" DS Robson said smugly.

"Who told you that?" DS Carruthers said abruptly.

"It's all around the station, it's hot gossip, everyone knows you are bedding him." DS Robson said sardonically.

"So why did you come on to me?"

"To see if I could crack the case as well." DS Robson paused then laughed.

"What's a matter?" DC Kapoor interrupted. He had come back from the toilet.

"THIS CREEP!" DS Carruthers hollered. The detectives both made their way out of the Stag Inn, the other officers present stared in their direction.

"What was that all about?" DC Kapoor asked. DS Carruthers told him what was said,

"I'm happy with you, I don't want a sleaze like him."

"Do you want me to go back in there?" DC Kapoor said angrily.

"No leave it!"

They walked purposely towards the local taxi rank.

"Do you fancy going to our favourite Chinese restaurant?" DC Kapoor asked.

"Yeah, I'm starving."

The meal was lovely as usual. Faith and Vikram walked back to her home on Ivy Street. Faith's house was in total darkness. She opened the front door and put the hall light on. She took off her high heels and went into the kitchen to make them a hot cup of coffee. She had been only gone a few seconds when Faith screamed hysterically. Vikram ran to her aid.

"Look, Look." Faith pointed.

"What is it?" Vikram asked.

"It's Pickles." Faith cried, she put her hand to her mouth.

Faith's ginger tom had been dismembered on her kitchen chopping board. Pickles head had been severed and he was slashed down the middle of his stomach. Blood and entrails were all to see. On the kitchen wall was written 'SLUT' in Pickle's blood. Faith was a complete mess; she was in floods of tears.

Vikram pulled her towards him and wrapped his loving safe arms around her. She stuck to him like glue. Her sobs were muffled. Vikram escorted her to the lounge and made her comfy on the sofa. He then poured her an Irish whiskey from the crystal decanter.

"I'm going to call this in Faith." Vikram said.

"No, don't please."

"This is bad, what if you were on your own here. I would be finding you dead in the morning." DC Kapoor was adamant.

"No, I don't want anyone involved." Faith shouted. Vikram didn't listen he phoned the police station and reported the incident. He went into the lounge,

"They are on their way."

"You shouldn't have done that?" Faith concluded. Vikram kissed her on her head.

"Everything is going to be OK." Vikram insisted.

"I hope so?" Faith managed a smile.

Vikram poured them both a glass of whiskey from the decanter.

He nudged her knee. She looked up gradually, she looked a sight, her mascara had run down her cheeks. He passed her the drink.

"How did they get in?" Faith said inaudibly.

"The French doors in the dining room have been forced open." Vikram replied.

"It's got to be Ronnie, all this Psychological shit!"

"Why did they write SLUT in Pickles blood on the kitchen wall." Vikram asked. Faith looked up ashamed.

"They have been watching you and me coming in and going from here. I am sorry, but they must have torched your car. They are not going to stop until I drop the case against him." Faith cried.

"You can tell me anything you know?" Vikram took a seat next to her on the sofa. Faith looked into his eyes.

"Ronnie was a lovely guy when we first met, he wined and dined me, sent me flowers constantly at home and at work. He made me feel very special. Ronnie was 14 years older than me and I suppose that was the attraction. A father figure. Ronnie had been married before so we had our ceremony in Luton Town Registry office. It was a great day, and then we had a two-week honeymoon in Roatan, Honduras. He knew I always wanted go. I had seen the place on a holiday program on Sky. It was a beautiful experience. We were so in love. For years it was good then it started going downhill. He had always had a tendency to feel jealous.

We went to my best friend's birthday bash in Milton Keynes. He had gone to the bar to get some drinks when a guy came over to dance with me. I dint mind, but when I got back to my seat Ronnie was fuming at me. At the end of the night the guy who I danced with was standing outside having a cigarette. I didn't see it coming. Ronnie attacked him and broke his nose. The Police were called, but we fled the scene. That was the first time, but not the last that I saw his anger. On the way home in the taxi, Ronnie said I encouraged him and it was my fault he fought with him. Then he dramatically changed towards me, especially when I couldn't bare him a son or daughter. We couldn't have IVF treatment because Ronnie had too many debts…Like I said he was married before; he had a daughter with her. But she moved down to Cornwall with her mum and he hardly saw her. Now I know why she left Luton….Ronnie put a tracker on my phone he was convinced I was seeing someone else. He slowly, but surely chipped away at my self-esteem, rubbishing me, telling me I was fat, useless and ugly. He monitored what I wore, he even checked my knickers daily to see if I had sex while I was out. He knew I had no family nearby, he stopped me seeing my friends and when I was not at work, he would not let me out. He made threats to my life If I did not behave."

"So, you were in a coercive relationship?" Vikram said angrily.

"Did he physically hurt you?"

"Only towards the end of the relationship, when he was drunk, he would use me as a punch bag. By this time, he had destroyed all the love I had for him. Ronnie was a control freak, possessive and a jealous bastard." Faith sobbed. Vikram put his arm around her and held her tight.

"Ronnie raped me on several occasions because I would not sleep with him. I was petrified of him. I thought he would kill me. I knew I had to leave him. I packed my suitcase and I was going to move into an apartment in Stopsley, Luton. But came home early and caught me leaving. He went crazy, he was a monster, I was frightened. He pinned me up against the kitchen wall, he throttled me, I was so scared, I was gasping for air, I came around on the floor and he had taken off my knickers and he raped me again. I went to work in a black polo neck jumper to hide the bruises, but I broke down at work and I don't know how I got the courage, but it all came out. My superiors were shocked, Ronnie was a fellow officer, a Detective Inspector. Later that day he was arrested. I felt ashamed."

"I will protect you; I won't let him do anything to you again." Vikram held her tightly.

"Thanks Vikram." Faith sobbed. She fell asleep in his arms.

There was a knock at the door. DI Read and two uniformed officers stood there.

"Hiya DC Kapoor, I understand some body has broken in and disassembled DS Carruthers cat. Is DS Carruthers here?"

"I will wake her up then I will show you the kitchen." Vikram said. DI Read nodded.

"This is terrible, I've never seen anything like this before." DI Read said.

"No, it's not very nice. DS Carruthers is heartbroken." DC Kapoor replied.

"I'm not surprised…I will phone SOCO and I will take a statement from you both."

They went and sat in the lounge the two uniformed went outside to their patrol car. DS Carruthers appeared fresh faced she had been to the bathroom to compose herself. DS Carruthers told him about her husband and her transfer from Luton CID. DI Read assumed the other break-in and the torching of DC Kapoor car was all connected. DI Read made plenty of notes and said he would contact DCI Barnes in the morning and make him aware of what's been going on. The DS and DC both said thank you and DI Read assured them that this incident would be kept quiet from everyone's hears.

"Can you make sure those clowns in the patrol car know that too? They are responsible for spreading mine and Faith's relationship around the Police Station."

"Ok, I will sort it…I'm going to the drive through I've not eaten seen earlier, hopefully SOCO will be here when get back."

7 am.

SOCO had concluded their investigation. Everything was catalogued and photographed, there was definitely a Psycho on the loose. Upstairs had never been touched, so Faith had gone to bed. Vikram lay on the sofa in-case he was needed. He had already planned that after SOCO had finished that he was going to clean-up the kitchen and bury Pickles in the back garden.

CHAPTER TWENTY-THREE
Saturday 24th December 2016
Christmas Eve

Faith waited for Vikram in the Coffee House on the High Street in Stowgarth Town Centre. Faith was a blithering wreck and she was trying to keep it together. The demise of old Pickles her faithful companion had hit her hard. Who would do a thing like that? Someone was frightening her, hoping it would stop her giving evidence against her husband.

Faith sat next to the full-length window in a brown leather tub armchair. It had a smooth curved back and thick wooden legs. There was a low dark coffee table with a glass top for easy cleaning. She had already ordered the drinks, but they had not arrived at the table yet. Faith gazed out the window on to the High Street. DC Windass was stood in the doorway of the chemist. He was met by Stowgarth FM Australian DJ, she knew it was him because he had been in the local gazette. He was the DJ at a Christmas Charity event at the Town Hall. Another guy was with him. Faith had an instinctive feeling about this, she retrieved her mobile from her coat pocket and filmed what was going on.

DC Windass and Cody Scott stood talking for a couple of minutes then Cody Scott gave him a fat envelope, it looked like it was full of money. They shook hands, DC Windass turned and headed down the High Street and Cody and his mate walked the other way.

A lanky young lad, with severe acne came to the tables with their drinks. Vikram had just come back from doing some shopping. He didn't believe in the birth of Jesus, as he was Sikh, but he had brought Faith a present.

"I've found out who's our leak at the station." Faith said proudly.

"Who is it?"

"DC Windass."

"You're Joking." Vikram looked in amazement.

"I wish I was."

Faith showed him the footage on her mobile phone.

"I've sent a message and the video to DCI Barnes, he said he will deal with it when we go back to work after Christmas." Faith said smugly, "Did you get what you wanted from the shops." She enquired, "Is that mine?" She pointed to pink and purple bag, "Can I have a look?"

"No, you will have to wait until tomorrow." Vikram replied. Faith bent over and kissed him.

"What's that for?" Vikram blushed.

"Thank you for burying Pickles and cleaning the kitchen. There's no way I could have done it."

"That's fine, don't worry…At least our superiors know about it and is investigating the matter in hand."

Cody Scott had been beaten up and had been eating hospital food for last few days. He was glad to be home. He was now off work until the New Year. His assistant had taken over the early and evening shows and was doing a fantastic job. Cody Scott had a prang of jealousy, because she was doing so well. Cody Scott was in Stowgarth Town Centre with his boyfriend Archie Weir. They had been together a couple of years. Archie Weir played for Stowgarth Town Football Club. Everyone knew he was gay, but he was a very good goalkeeper in his early career he had trials with Lincoln City. Archie Weir was 27, six years younger than his lover. He was medium height and built like a trojan horse. He had a mop of messy brown hair with sapphire blue eyes. He wore small diamond earrings and he was covered in tattoos. He was a good-looking man but like Cody Scott, he knew it.

Before coming into town, they had done some last-minute food shopping at a well-known foreign supermarket in Cheadley Heath. They weaved in and out of shops on the High Street bumping into people who were overwhelmed with joy that their favourite disk jockey was out of hospital even though he looked battered and bruised. He looked down at his gold watch. It was 4.00pm.

"I know you have not been well. I thought I was going to lose you. I've arranged for a table at Bellissimo. It's for 5pm. We're going to be early, but we can have a few drinks before in the lounge bar." Archie Weir announced.

"Is that why you didn't want to come into town in the car?"

"That was kinda the plan." Archie Weir laughed.

The two men with their many bags walked in the direction of the Italian Restaurant. Bellissimo was on Chaucer Street just off the High Street. They were crossing over the High Street when Cody Scott froze, his colour drained into the gutter.

"What's the matter? It looks like you have seen a ghost?" Archie Weir asked with concern.

"That's the lad that who attacked me." Cody Scott pointed to a tall wiry lad with a black bandana and messy ginger hair.

"Are you sure?"

"Damn right I am." Cody Scott insisted. Archie was furious, but the two men followed him from a safe distance.

The lad looked like he was meeting someone he kept looking at his mobile phone. Archie filmed the footage on his iPhone hoping to pick up a clue of his identity. If he was a known criminal around Stowgarth the police would have known him. The lad disappeared down a side street; Chaucer Street. When they caught up with him, he was standing outside 'Bellissimo.' They stood behind a blue transit van out of sight. They glanced in his direction. The lad looked down at his mobile phone again. The entrance door of 'Bellissimo' opened and Hugo Molinari appeared. He shook the lads' hand and hurried him inside the restaurant. Moments later the lad with the black bandana appeared, he walked down the street towards them. He was rather pleased with himself as he counted a wad of money. Cody Scott was dumbstruck; he could not believe what he was seeing. He felt sickened to the core, he thought they were best friends. But Why? He was perplexed. Archie Weir wanted to go and confront Cody Scott's so called best mate, but his boyfriend asked him to leave it.

"Shall we call the police and tell them what we know and show them the footage on my phone." Archie asked.

Cody Scott was still in shock. He was immovable.

"It's Christmas Eve, I don't want to ruin Hugo's boys Christmas. I will ring the Police, but not until the day after boxing day."

"Don't you think he deserves to have his life turned upside down?"

"Not at Christmas. There might be a valid reason? It might not have anything to do with the attack?"

"You're puddled, you live in fantasy world." Archie was very annoyed. Cody Scott was blind to Hugo's faults; he had put him on a high pedestal for the last ten years.

The two men walked towards the taxi rank. They did not have to wait long for a taxi to pull up and take them home. Cody Scott was very quiet, he thought: *We have been friends for the last ten years. I can't believe he would do this to me? Why did he want to hurt me? What did I do to deserve it?* Cody

Scott looked out the window, tears were falling down his face.

Faith and Vikram went to the Stowgarth Royal Playhouse to watch this year's pantomime. It was Cinder-fella. Nobody famous was staring, but it was a great production. Vikram was new to the experience, but for Faith it was an annual occurrence. She was a big kid at heart. Faith's father took her every year from the age of five until she was a teenager. He died of a massive heart attack and she was left devastated. She never knew her mum she died in child birth. Faith moved in with her grandmother and she took over the parental responsibility until she was eighteen. She was in her late eighties a tough old bird. She died of old age when Faith had been accepted into the Police Force at the age of 23. Every Christmas she went to her local theatre and watched the pantomime production in remembrance of the special time she spent with her father.

When it had finished, everybody dashed down the main stairs into the cream marble polished lobby and out into the freezing cold. Faith looked at her watch and asked if Vikram fancied having a quiet drink before they got a taxi to Sandwell. It was DI Love's retirement party. The piano bar was very lavish compared to the interval bar. A tall, attractive man dressed in a black and white suit showed them to a table.

"It is waitress service only. Would you like to browse the food and drink menu? If you're wanting wine, I recommend the house red or white they are both beautiful."

"I would like a bottle of house red." Faith replied.

"I will have a tomato juice." Vikram added.

"That's adventurous." Faith giggled like a school girl.

"I will inform your waitress and she will bring your drinks over. Have a good evening."

They both sat quietly at the table,

"I am glad you have decided to stay over for Christmas. What have you told your fiancé?" Faith asked.

"They think I am staying with a colleague because we both are on-call over Christmas."

"Well, that's the truth." Faith smiled, "You seem preoccupied, are you ok?"

"The wedding is off; Chadda is going back to her family in India."

"Why?"

"My family wanted me to be a husband and father, but that's not for me. Chadda realised that the job meant everything to me and she would always be number two."

"I'm sorry to hear that." Faith lied. She changed the subject, "I suppose it's normally a quiet time for you and your family during Christianity festivities."

"Sikhs do not celebrate the birth of Jesus Christ they use this time to engage in charitable activities and spend time with family."

"What is your stance on drinking alcohol?" Faith asked.

"Baptised Sikhs are forbidden from drinking, but some non-baptised Sikhs do consume alcohol."

"What is your stance on eating meat?" Faith probed again.

"Sikhs can eat meat as long as the animals are not killed in a religious ceremony and do not suffer long, painful deaths. Eating meat is not a requirement or prohibited for Sikhs, but a personal choice. Most Sikhs do eat meat and drink, and this does not affect their status as Sikhs…I choose to eat a vegetarian diet, like I choose not drink Alcohol."

"Luckily, we have nut roast for Christmas dinner tomorrow." Faith smiled.

Vikram reached for Faith's hand and gently squeezed it. She knew what he was thinking about and the feeling was a hundred percent mutual.

They drank their drinks and Vikram paid the bill. The melee in the lobby had now eased. Some excited children and their parents were starting to queue for the evening show. Faith and Vikram exited the building and walked in the direction of the taxi rank. It was bitterly cold. Faith wondered if it was going to snow again.

The Cross Keys was very busy, the party was in the lounge. It had been decorated lovely for Christmas, but it did not hide the drab yellow walls and distressed paintwork. It was a shame because the seating, furnishings and carpet were in good condition. DI Love was pleased to see them. He handed them both a glass of Bucks Fizz on their arrival.

"This is quite nice." DC Kapoor said, "What is it?"

"It's fresh orange and cheap champagne." DS

Carruthers replied, turning her nose up at it.

"Wow, it's bloody lovely." DC Kapoor guzzled it down fast; the bubbles tickled his nose.

DS Carruthers and DC Kapoor scanned the room for somewhere to sit. There were a lot of family and friends. Her fellow detectives were sitting at a large rectangle table. DCI Barnes sat at the head of the table with his beautiful wife. She wore a long red A-line party dress. She looked much younger than her husband. You would never have guessed she had given birth to three children. Her husband was outnumbered he had a house full of females. They were all grown up now and had children of their own. His five grandchildren were all girls. Three of her male colleagues were sitting with their very attractive girlfriends. DC Windass was amongst them, he nudged the other detectives to alert them to their presence.

"I told you he was bedding her." He said quietly. The others cracked up laughing.

"She must be twenty years older than him; it would be like shagging your mother-in-law." DC Windass continued. The three detective constables had been drinking since they had finished their Christmas Eve round of golf.

DS Carruthers and DC Kapoor sat next to DC

Booth and her boyfriend.

He was tall and thin. He looked the spitting image of a well-known boy band member. DC Matthews faced them in his wheelchair, he still didn't look well, but he wanted to be there.

The DJ was DI Love's nephew. He was just legal to drink, but he looked younger. He was tall and had a spotty complexion. He was doing the music as a present for his uncle's retirement. He was doing a fantastic job. DS Carruthers and DC Kapoor found themselves the talk of the party. DC Windass could not stop sniggering behind their backs. To the disgruntlement of DCI Barnes. Suddenly DC Brookes shouted,

"LOOK WHO IT IS? LATE AGAIN DS MUNRO." There was a roar from detectives gathered around the table.

Moments later they were all joined by DCS Hargreaves and his wife.

She was small and round. She looked a lot older than her husband. DCS Hargreaves was suited and booted for the occasion. Everyone was on their best behaviour because of his presence, but it soon evaporated when he brought everyone a drink.

An hour later, DS Carruthers was stood at the

bar, she was joined by a tipsy DC Windass.

"Are you and lover boy enjoying yourselves tonight?" DC Windass said boldly.

"What is your problem? If I was you, I should shut up or I will show this mobile footage of you taking money from DJ Cody Scott outside 'Boots the chemist' earlier today to DCS Hargreaves who is stood over there."

"But…" DC Windass stumbled.

"You're going to say you're a friend of his, you're not, you're the station's leak."

DC Windass got his round of drinks and sheepishly went back to his table.

The party was not banging, but everyone was having a good time. Everyone had clubbed together for DI Love's present. They had paid for a full year's membership at his prestigious Golf Club in Grayson. Larry was overwhelmed with the gift.

Larry had ordered a cortege of taxi cabs to take his guest's home. Because it was Christmas Eve, Larry could not get an extension. So, it closed at its normal time. DC Kapoor was a little drunk, he wasn't used to drinking alcohol. DS Carruthers wasn't as drunk as usual. She bundled him into a taxi and they were escorted back home.

CHAPTER TWENTY-FOUR
Sunday 25th December 2016   Christmas Day.

Christmas Day had been fabulous, waking up with the man she was falling in love with. Faith brought him breakfast in bed, he was overwhelmed with the gesture. She had also brought their Christmas presents from under the tree up to the bedroom. They unwrapped them together. Vikram had brought Faith a Pandora bracelet with charms. She loved it. Ronnie her estranged husband didn't do Christmas. He was a scrooge as well as a rapist. Faith had brought Vikram a 2017 black leather Filofax. His old one was battered, but he still took it everywhere with him. He seemed chuffed enough. They both kissed and ended up making love.

Vikram watched the Christmas music channel in the lounge. While Faith prepared the Christmas dinner. He wasn't struck on the Christmas number one. But Faith loved it. Soon as she heard it coming from the lounge's television, she strolled in singing and dancing. She couldn't hold a tune bless her.

The nut roast and Christmas pudding with Irish Whiskey sauce was amazing. They even pulled a cracker and wore those silly coloured paper hats. In the afternoon they watched some animated film and a repeat of a long-ago Christmas comedy special.

Faith was guzzling red wine and Vikram was slowly drinking the Bucks Fizz. He knew it had a small amount of alcohol, but that didn't bother him.

"Are you going to tell DCI Barnes and DI Read about us?" Vikram asked.

"Well, to be honest, I think they would have gathered by last night's performance by DC Windass and company…"

"Do you think they will separate us?"

"More than likely, but we already guessed that would happen if they found out?"

"What time is your niece coming tomorrow?" Vikram probed again.

"Knowing her it will be early. She's bringing her car and her husband will be driving his…I know I'm buying her car off her, I know that car will be in good condition, but will you look over it for me."

"Of course." Vikram insisted.

"I know you don't mind ferrying me about, but it will give me some independence. And it's going cheap, because I'm having it." Faith smiled.

"What kind of car is it?" Vikram enquired.

"Not sure. I know it's red in colour." Faith giggled.

Vikram loved it when she was relaxed, but he knew there was an underlining issue. The stalking, breaking and entering was making her nervous coming home and being alone.

The day went without a hitch, and they both enjoyed the day together. They cuddled and lay together on the sofa, they laughed into the late into the evening.

Monday 26th December 2016, Boxing Day

Faith had got up bright and early that morning. She left Vikram in bed, but he was washed and dressed for when Faith's niece and family arrived.

Faith's niece, her husband and two boys arrived from Kings Lynn.

Vikram was worried how they were going to react when they saw a tall Indian man in a black turban. All his worries were extinguished, they totally accepted him. Faith had brought the boys a Norwich City FC home shirt.

While Faith was left speaking to her niece and her husband. Vikram joined the boys in the garden and they played football.

Faith did a Christmas dinner; she had brought a large turkey crown and Vikram had some of yesterday's nut roast. Faith had a tear run down her cheek, but before anybody saw her, she wiped it away. They all sat around the dinner table and enjoyed the food that had been cooked. Faith had thought how nice it was to have her family around her table, well the ones she cared about. It also went through her mind, Sandra de Villiers adored Christmas, but she would never see one again and sadly they still haven't found her murderer.

After the meal the men went to have a look at Faith's new car. Vikram was surprised to see a 2010 red Sports car. It was in fantastic condition.

"Can I ask why you are selling this car?" Vikram asked.

"I'm working from home now and having two cars just doesn't make sense." The niece's husband said.

"These cars were totally underestimated when they first came out. I can't wait to get my new car tomorrow night."

"I thought this green car was yours?"

"No, it's a courtesy car." Vikram told him what had happened to his car.

Vikram took the car for a drive around the block. He was very impressed; it drove lovely and purred like a cat. They went back inside.

"What do you think?" Faith asked.

"It's beautiful, if I wasn't getting my new car tomorrow. I would ditch the courtesy car and drive this one."

"Well, that's a yes." Her niece stated, "So, you will have two cars?"

"The reason I wanted a car was because I didn't feel independent, I was depending on Vikram. So, we talked then I remembered about you selling your car. That's why I asked you."

"Are you sure you only want three grand?" Faith asked.

"Yes, that's what we agreed, here's the log book, MOT and its fully service history. We always took it back to the dealer, but it's up to you."

Faith's relatives stayed a couple more hours, before driving back home.

Faith and Vikram took the car out for a drive. Faith loved it. They went to the 'The Black Swan Inn' in Redmile. It was next to the river stow. The Inn was mainly a summer place where you would bring your family and have a picnic by the river and feed the ducks. Faith and Vikram sat at a table in the piano bar, everywhere else was busy with customers. Faith had a bottle of red wine and Vikram had something non-alcoholic because he was going to drive them back to Cheadley Heath. The young Pianist was really good. Faith was pleased when he did some George Michael & Wham songs. But she did not know the significance of the medley at that time. Faith was not very warm; Vikram spotted a table next to the open fire. So, they moved. They sat down and enjoyed the warmth of the burning coal fire.

They talked and talked, laughed and laughed, and that's what they were good at. Vikram made Faith so happy. But she was worried what Ronnie or his henchmen was going to do next.

CHAPTER TWENTY-FIVE
Tuesday 27th December 2016

DS Carruthers looked at her digital clock on the dashboard of her new car. It was 7.30pm. She was going to be early for work. The cold weather had returned. The roads were frostbitten and the pavements glistened in the car headlights. DS Carruthers beeped her horn at the old black Range Rover Vogue in front of her.

It was driving far too slowly and it was taking up two lanes of traffic. DS Carruthers eventually navigated her way around it, the one-way system around town was just hectic. She got stranded in a queue of traffic. There had been an accident on the High Street. A 2008 blue Japanese car had smashed into the back of a brand-new red transit van. All the passengers were conscious, but dazed. As she approached, she thought she might have to stop to help, but an ambulance and a traffic car had just arrived at the scene. DS Carruthers was bumper to bumper with the car in front. Now, she knew she was going to be late again. DS Carruthers mind wandered as she held the steering wheel. *I had a fantastic festive period and a well-earned break. Then I found out on the television that George Michael had sadly died on Christmas day at his home in London. I was devastated. He had been my favourite popstar since my early childhood. In my bedroom I listened and sang his music, often loud and out of tune. I had posters of him and Andrew Ridgley emblazoned all over my walls. I even had a matching duvet set. George Michael was my idol. I was very upset, but I did not want it to spoil my festive cheer.*

A car beeped behind her waking her from her wandering thoughts. The row of vehicles in front of her had surged forward and she was holding up the traffic. Faith tried to move forward, but her handbrake was stuck. She suddenly had a rush of panic and embarrassment. She could see the drivers flapping behind her in her rear mirror. It took all her force to release it. Once she had caught up with the cars in front, she was bumper to bumper all the way to the Police Station.

Luckily everyone was sitting around talking. DCI Barnes or the DI Read had not started the morning briefing yet. She looked towards the DCI's office, but there was no one there.

"Where's the boss?" DS Carruthers said perplexed.

"He's behind you." DC Windass bellowed like he was in the audience in a pantomime. Faith looked behind her and saw DCS Hargreaves glaring at her. She gulped.

"Sorry Sir." DS Carruthers felt embarrassed.

She thought *Twice in one flipping morning*.

"I will listen to your excuses when the short briefing is over…and DC Windass please grow-up." The DCS snapped.

"I hope you all have a good Christmas. As you may have guessed DCI Barnes is not here today. He is on compassionate leave and will be back tomorrow. It is DI Read's first official day, so I am here to observe." He handed the reins to DI Read.

"I hope you all had a good Christmas. We are re-starting the Stowgarth armed robberies and the Sandra de Villiers investigations. The investigation teams personnel are staying the same, but I would like to speak to DS Carruthers afterwards." DI Read kept it short and sweet and ended the short briefing. DCS Hargreaves stood next to the coffee machine. He caught DS Carruthers eye, "I need to see you." She followed him to his makeshift office.

"Shut the door behind you." He raised his voice an octave higher. She was expecting a roasting.

"May I ask why you was 10 minutes late?"

"I left home at 7.15am I got into the town centre about 7.30am, but the roads around

Stowgarth were chaotic. There was a road traffic accident then it was bumper to bumper all the way here." DS Carruthers said honestly. She thought *This is the first time I've been late since I've been here. Why don't you pick on DS Munro she is always late and never gets told off.* "I'm sorry if I was late and it won't happen again." She growled.

"I accept your excuse that the traffic around town was busy because I got caught up in it too. I get here on time for every shift. Me and you sing from the same hymn sheet, I've only brought you in here to make a statement to them out there in the Incident room. That lateness is not acceptable." He paused, "I understand DI Read wants to speak to you." The DCS waved to catch DI Reads attention. Moments later he entered the room. He took a seat facing them both.

"There are two things? Sandra de Villiers funeral is tomorrow at 11am. It is at Stowgarth Catholic Church then she is being buried in the Edenfield Road cemetery on the Halstead Estate. And I spoke to DCI Barnes earlier this morning and he wants me to split up you and DC Kapoor. This is only because of your relationship…You can choose who you would like to work with DC Dempster or DC Dimka?" DI Read asked.

"To be honest I would like to work with DC Dempster again. I find him to be a very fine detective." DS Carruthers replied.

"Ok, DC Kapoor can work with DC Dimka."

"What's happening about DC Windass?" DC Carruthers asked.

"Well, thanks for your footage. I have seen it and it is damning evidence that he is the stations leak…The Radio station is going to get a visit too. We will be questioning him shortly and I will be suspending him until is hearing in the New Year."

"What do you think will happen?" DS Carruthers asked.

"He will be dismissed; the hierarchy here won't accept this behaviour."

DCS Hargreaves announced.

DC Windass had been called into the office; you could hear DCS Hargreaves giving him the riot act. DS Carruthers was briefing her investigation team. When DC Windass appeared red-faced and extremely pissed off. He strolled with purpose over to the gathered detectives.

"Thanks a lot SERG!" He boomed.

"What's the matter?" DC Dempster asked.

"I've been suspended and I'm going to lose my job."

"You have only yourself to blame." DS Carruthers stated.

DC Windass got his coat and marched out of the Incident room. DS Carruthers announced the changes.

"Why has he been suspended?" DC Dempster asked.

"I can't tell you why? But you will find out in due course."

The detectives were still gathered around DS Carruthers desk when DC
Booth appeared,

"I've just had a phone call from a Mrs Derbyshire. She doesn't normally read the local rag, but she was spending Christmas with her family in New Marsh. Anyway, the Gazette had a picture of unknown man slipping and sliding along Church Street. Well, she thinks it's her neighbour Mr Clive Williams."

"He might have seen our killer?" DC Dempster said with excitement.

"What's the address DC Booth?" DS Carruthers asked.

"It's number four Colne Close, on the Halstead Estate. I've checked his name through the electoral role and it's right. I've done a quick criminal record check and he has no previous."

"Thank you, DC Booth." DS Carruthers praised her. She turned to the detectives, "Me and DC Dempster will go and see Mr Williams. You two can stay behind you have plenty of work to do…"

The traffic around Stowgarth was busy, but it did not take them long to find Colne Close, it was just off the Edenfield Road. The properties on the close were all old pensioner bungalows. They were all built by the council, they were all brick and very modern. The detectives arrived on the doorstep, DC Dempster rang the doorbell, a man medium size and weight answered the door. He was in his late sixties; he was a lot older than Charlie Whelan had described. He had grey thick hair; hazel eyes and he was clean shaven. He was wearing dark blue cardigan and brown corduroy trousers.

"How can I help? If you're trying to sell me something then don't both wasting your time." He said.

The detectives introduced themselves and showed their warrant cards.

"Sorry you better come in; we get a lot of cold callers here."

The detectives were shown into a stifling warm bungalow. The lounge was quite small. The detectives were asked to take a seat on the floral sofa and Mr Williams took a seat facing them in a wingback chair. The lounge was very tidy, the walls were painted magnolia. There were two large wooden bookcases full of books and vinyl records. There was also an old standing-up piano leaning against one of the walls.

"This is my cat, she is an old dear like me, but sadly she is not very friendly with strangers." Mr Williams pointed out.

The cat lay on a small clean pink bed in front of the roaring fire. The cat was a lilac point Siamese. She looked at the detectives like they were invading her space.

"Can I ask? have you been watching or listening to the local news regarding the murder of a local woman." DS Carruthers asked.

"I am sorry, I did, but I am a self-confessed

bookworm. As you can see, I don't have a television. I either play the piano or I play my records on my record player. I do listen to the news on the radio, but sometimes it becomes a bit monotonous. It's always full of doom and gloom."

"Where were you on Friday 16th December 2016 between 4pm and 6pm?"

"It was at the Rotary Club of Stowgarth's Christmas Party. It began at 12pm and ended just after 4pm. I was going to get a taxi home, but I was not the only one who had the idea. So, I decided to walk home in the heavy snow."

"What route did you take home?" DS Carruthers asked.

"Well, I wish I had never started walking. The snow was thicker than I first thought. The high street was perilous. I was slipping and sliding all over the place. As I turned on to church street the snow and ice got no better. It took me ages to get home. I was worried about my cat, but she was nice and warm in her bed."

"The reason we are asking is that Sandra de Villiers was murdered in the Catholic Church Carpark at about the same time you were slipping and sliding along church street…Did you see anybody hanging around church street and the church carpark?"

"I saw a car come out the carpark then I didn't see anybody until I got onto Gorton Road. A man rushed straight past me with a mobile phone stuck to his ear."

"Can you describe the man?" DS Carruthers asked.

"He was half my age, tall, slender. He wore a long trench coat and one of those silly hats…and he wore ski glasses."

"What time did you arrive home?"

"When I arrived home my phone was ringing. It was my daughter. It must have been around a quarter to six, because she rings me at the same time every night. She was annoyed I had walked home in the snow. Ever since I have had this bloody cold." He laughed.

"We saw you on the town's CCTV slipping and sliding along the high street, but we lost you when you turned on to church street. I do believe what you are telling me, but I will have to speak to your daughter just to check she phoned at 5.45pm." DC Dempster said.

Mr Williams handed him his phone book and

DC Dempster wrote the number on his notepad and went outside to phone his daughter.

Moments later DC Dempster appeared,

"Your daughter confirms she rang you at 5.45pm on the day in question. There is one question I have?" He asked.

"Yes, what's that?"

"Are you a Norwich City supporter?"

"Yes, why? I'm a lifelong member."

"We saw you on the CCTV wearing a canary yellow and green woolly hat and scarf."

"I was born in Norfolk, I lived in Cromer. Everyone at my school supported them. I started supporting them when I was nine. I am now 69. It's been a long arduous ride." Mr Williams laughed.

"Well, I'm a Lincoln City supporter, I've seen the highs and lows. I should be happy we are top of the National League…Let's see if we get promoted to the football league at the end of the season." DC Dempster hoped and prayed.

"If the man you saw on Gorton Road is the murderer, would you be able to attend an identity parade."

"Definitely if it helps."

"Thanks for your help. It's been lovely meeting you." They all shook hands. The detectives were pleased with the outcome. Mr Williams was a really nice guy. DC Dempster drove them back to the station. They were disappointed they had not apprehended the murderer, but they were pleased they had eliminated him from their enquires.

The detectives got back to the Incident room; it was virtually empty. DC Kapoor was at his desk ploughing through emails and statements. DS Carruthers went to speak to DI Read in the DCI's office, but he wasn't there. DCS Hargreaves was sat at his desk.

"Hi, Sir, where is everyone?"

"There's been another armed robbery, this time at a newsagent, on Rossington Drive, Sandwell. The owner was beaten to a pulp."

DS Carruthers told him about their visit to Colne Close and the questioning of Mr Williams.

"We are missing the final piece to the puzzle. The killer is right under our nose." DS Carruthers announced boldly.

"I'm sure you will figure it out, you are a very good detective sergeant. I know you have not been here long. Why don't you apply for the new DI position, you have passed the detective inspector exam and I know you was up for promotion in the Luton CID. So, between you and me, you have a very good chance." DCS Hargreaves smiled.

"Thanks Sir, I will think about it…I'm going for lunch then I have some emails and statements to go through."

"As you wish, detective sergeant." DCS Hargreaves smiled, he gave DS Carruthers the creeps!!. She walked back into the Incident room."

CHAPTER TWENTY-SIX
Wednesday 28th December 2016
The Funeral

DS Carruthers thought *How ironic is it that Sandra de Villiers funeral is a stone's throw away from where she was brutally murdered in the church carpark.*

The church was packed with mourners. Sandra de Villiers was in her open mahogany coffin at the foot of the churches naïve. She must have been a very well-liked individual because both sides of the aisle were full of relatives and friends. The detectives stood at the back of the church next to the entrance.

DS Carruthers had forewarned her fellow detective that the requiem mass was long and drawn out especially to a non-Catholic person.

Johan de Villiers was sat in the old wooden pews at the front of the church. He was sat next to an elderly couple. DS Carruthers assumed they were Sandra's parents.

"Do you think the killer is here?" DC Dempster whispered.

"More than likely, if its someone who knew

her, they will want to be showing their grief to the world." DS Carruthers replied quietly under her breath.

Johan de Villiers did the eulogy. With Father Doyle's help he also planned and included Sandra's favourite hymns and bible readings. Father Doyle had known Sandra since she was a young girl, so he knew her very well. Probably better than her husband. Johan de Villiers spoke about Sandra's life and her accomplishments in and out of the show ring. DS Carruthers thought *After everything I have found out about Johan and Sandra's marriage was, he the right person to do the eulogy.*

Everyone who was Catholic celebrated mass while the others sat quietly in respect. DS Carruthers had not celebrated mass since her grandmother's funeral and she didn't intend to do it ever again. The funeral finished with the hymn 'abide by me'. Sandra mahogany coffin was carried out of the church to the awaiting horse drawn hearse. The burial was taking place in the Edenfield Road Cemetery on the Halstead estate. Only family and very close friends were in attendance. DS Munro was amongst them. A lot of people stayed behind in the church hall until they came back.

Everyone had returned to the church hall. Johan de Villiers introduced DS Carruthers and DC Dempster to Sandra's parents. The burial had been private, personal and very emotional. They asked how the investigation was going and implored them to find her killer.

Father Doyle said a few words then everyone tucked into the lavish buffet. Sandra hardly drank so there was tea, coffee and soft drinks available.

DS Carruthers and DC Dempster arrived back from the funeral. The incident room was eerie quiet. DCI Barnes was still on compassionate leave. DS Carruthers had been told by DS Read that his elderly mother had passed away over the Christmas period. She was told not to say anything to her fellow detectives. Only the senior detectives knew. DCS Hargreaves was in the office with DI Read. DC Matthews and DC Booth were working hard at their desks. DS Carruthers knocked on the office door. DI Read motioned for her to come in.

The superior officers were hunched together at the desk watching the laptop screen.

"How was the funeral?" DI Read asked.

"Very emotional for everyone present, but it was a nice funeral service."

"Good, I'm glad it went well."

"Are you watching yesterday's CCTV

footage of the robbery at the Newsagents?"

"Yes, come and have a look." DCS Hargreaves directed.

The robbery had the same M.O. as the other robberies around the Stowgarth area. There were two armed robbers, one was tall and one was small, the same as before. They were dressed the same and they were carrying shotguns. It showed the violent assault on the shop keeper. Then they left by the shop door, the camera picked up the getaway car parked on and off the pavement.

"DI Read, can you go back to the violent assault on the shop keeper please." DS Carruthers insisted.

The tall armed robber hits Mr Sharma with the butt of the shotgun. He falls to the floor and the armed robbers kicks and punches Mr Sharma. The daughter tries to pull him off her dad, in doing so she pulls at the neck of the armed robber's black jacket. A tattoo of a flower is revealed on his neck.

"Enlarge the picture of the tattoo, I bet it's a arum lily?" It appeared on the screen, "I know precisely who is behind these robberies."

"Enlighten us?" DCS Hargreaves said excitedly.

"Richard Downing lives with Sandra de Villiers brother Daniel Hardy." DS Carruthers explained who he was and how she knew him and where they lived.

"Well done DS Carruthers, I will let DS Munro know when she comes back from lunch. It will be up to her and her team to look into it and make the arrest. I take it that Daniel Hardy is his accomplice in the CCTV footage?" DI Read asked.

"That's where I would lay my bet." DS Carruthers smiled.

"Fine police work." DCS Hargreaves said appraisingly.

"All I need to do now is find out who killed Sandra de Villiers?" DS Carruthers said adamantly.

Richard Downing and Daniel Hardy were arrested later that afternoon. There was cash and drugs stashed all over the house. The shotguns were finally found up in the loft of the property. They were made safe by the ballistics team and taken away for forensic inspection. The two men were held in custody for the night before questioning the following day.

CHAPTER TWENTY-SEVEN
Thursday 29th October 2016

DS Carruthers got to the incident room early that morning. The DCI was back on duty, he was sat in his office with DI Read. When he saw her, he beckoned her to his office.

"Morning gents?" DS Carruthers said in a chirpy mood.

"Good morning." The senior officers said in unison.

"DS Carruthers, I take it, I have you to congratulate for solving the armed robberies investigation. The evidence is damning, DI Read and DS Munro will be questioning and charging them later today…I've spoken to DI Read and he tells me that you have been experiencing some personal issues. The three of us know that you were transferred here on the quiet from Luton CID not the Norwich Serious Crime Unit. And us three know why? DI Read has some interesting information." DCI Barnes concluded.

"I have spoken to DCI Bloom at the Luton CID. You will be pleased to know that your husband is still behind bars and from what she gathers off the streets and in the Luton CID that his associates aren't interested in intimidating you, because they have disassociated themselves from your husband."

"Who torched DC Kapoor brand new car and dissembled my beautiful male cat?" DS Carruthers wanted to get out of the room before she let her guard slip and cried. DC Kapoor was the only person she showed her true emotions too.

"Well, it's a bit of a mystery, but we will get there." DI Read said.

"I know I split you and DC Kapoor, but I have no choice, but put you both together today. DC Dempster and DC Dimka have phoned in sick with this mystery bug and with no DC Windass it just leaves you two." DCI Barnes interrupted."

"Yes, Guv."

Both of the Senior detectives sensed she was a little fragile, who wouldn't be after finding out that they had nothing to go on. Nothing led to her husband, but she was being intimidating and she was scared it was going to get a lot worse.

DS Carruthers kissed her Senior detective's feet and walked back into the incident room. DS Carruthers went straight to the drinks machine for a double expresso coffee. DC Kapoor joined her. She told him the good news; he was pleased as punch.

"I have some gossip for you. I overheard DS Munro complaining to DC Brookes that she might, meaning you, have solved this case, but she can't even solve my friends murder investigation." DC Kapoor said.

"Well, I'm not surprised. I've taken the limelight off her, between me and you DCS Hargreaves is not happy with her continual lateness and you know him he will stamp his authority before he retires."

Suddenly DS Munro walked back into the incident room. She had been to the canteen to grab the Senior detectives a bacon and sausage toasted sandwich.

"Good morning DS Carruthers and you DC Kapoor."

"Good morning." They said in unison.

"The two-faced cow." DS Carruthers said under her breath. She just glared at DC Kapoor. The psychic energy between them was palpable.

The briefing was short and sweet. DCI Barnes thanked DS Munro and her team for working endlessly on the armed robbery case. There was no doubt they had got the culprits and they would be questioned and charged later today. DCI

Barnes did not say much about the Sandra de Villiers case, other than it was moving in the right direction and for the next day or so they would be under-manned. DS Carruthers put her hand up in the air.

"Yes, DS Carruthers."

"Can me and DC Kapoor speak to Daniel Hardy before his questioning. It's not about the armed robbery case, it's solely to do with his sister's murder. It's really important to the investigation. If he is charged, he might not be so eager to talk to us."

"Yes, that's fine. I will send the Custody Sergeant an email explaining the situation and I'm sure if he does not allow it, I can speak to DCS Hargreaves."

A custody officer brought Daniel Hardy to the empty interview room in the custody suite. He stood outside until the arranged questioning was over. Daniel Hardy sat at the table. He shook from head to toe. The detectives sat facing him.

"This is not to do with your arrest. I want to ask you a question about your sister. We are recording you; we will be monitored by our CCTV cameras. You said you saw Sandra on the night before she was murdered at your house. You said you ate pizza, watched television and shared some cocaine. Do you still stand by that?"

"Of course. She came around every Thursday since the beginning of November." Daniel insisted.

"Well, we have a statement from her husband that she was teaching at the Molinari Dance School." DS Carruthers announced.

"She fell out with Hugo Molinari the dance school owner and teacher. She didn't tell her husband about it."

"Do you know what the argument was about?" DS Carruthers continued.

"No, she never said, Mrs Swallow might know why?"

"Who is Mrs Swallow?" DC Kapoor interjected before DS Carruthers could even asked the question. She gave him a look to say I'm in charge here, so button it.

"She used to go to Sandra's ringcraft training group, but she getting too old now. Sandra goes around there on a Wednesday night for tea. They were very close.

"Do you know where Mrs Swallow lives?" DS Carruthers asked. DC Kapoor kept quiet beside her.

"I know she lives in a bungalow in Cheadley Heath that's all I know."

"Were you and Richard, Sandra's dealer?" Daniel kept silent.

"We found drugs and loads of cash in your house." DC Kapoor stated.

"She never paid for it. I gave her what she wanted as a thank you for getting me off the streets. She paid the bond and three month's rent up front for Balfour Street for me. I owed her a lot."

"Thanks for all your help."

We will need you to sign a statement of the facts. DC Kapoor will do that. Then the custody officer outside will take you back to your cell.

DS Carruthers went to her desk in the Incident room. She rang Samantha Mealing, but there was no answer, so she left her message to call her back.

DS Carruthers and DC Kapoor was sat next to PC Sanders. She tucked into a prawn salad baguette, DC Kapoor had vegetable risotto while PC Sanders was halfway through a plate of curry, rice and chips.

"Have you been busy?" DS Carruthers asked.

"Shoplifting is on the increase again in Stowgarth. I thought it might have died down now that Christmas is over. I have been to three incidents this morning, two in Stowgarth Town centre and one at ASDA in the retail park. They were all teenage girls." PC Sanders stated, "What about you two?"

"The Sandra de Villiers case is still on-going, but we are getting closer to finding the murderer. The spate of armed robberies in and around Stowgarth is coming to a conclusion." DS Carruthers replied.

"I understand you have the two culprits in custody?" PC Sanders asked.

"Where did you manage to find that out?" DS Carruthers replied.

"You know gossip flies around the station."

"Yes, we do…it's normally about us." DC Kapoor said adamantly. PC Sanders just grinned.

The detectives finished their food. DS Carruthers looked at the time on her mobile, she realised it was time to go back to the Incident room. They said goodbye and wandered back upstairs.

DS Carruthers was working at her desk when her internal phone rang making her jump out of her skin. It was Samantha Mealing.

"Hi DS Carruthers you phoned not so long ago, I was bathing one of my dogs, you asked me to ring you."

"Hiya Samantha. I'm wondering if you can help me? Do you have the contact address or telephone number for Mrs Swallow. I understand she attended your ringcraft training."

"I have those details somewhere, just hold on a minute." The phone went quiet. DS Carruthers could just hear dogs barking in the background. Then Samantha Mealing came back to the phone,

"It's 27 Delph Street, Cheadley heath and I've got her mobile phone number 070068428299."

"Thank you, Samantha, you have been a great help?" DS Carruthers put the phone down. She then made a call to Mrs Swallow and arranged to see her early that afternoon.

CHAPTER TWENTY-EIGHT

Mrs Swallow lived 20 minutes' walk from DS Carruthers home on Ivy Street. Number 27 Delph Street was a small-town house. At the front it had a small garden. There was a row of naked rose bushes and a small square lawn. DS Carruthers rang the doorbell. They could hear shuffling coming from inside, a few moments later a little elderly lady with a gnarled wooden walking stick answered the door.

"Hello I'm DS Carruthers and this DC Kapoor." The elderly lady looked baffled, "I spoke to you this morning on the phone."

"Oh yes, please come in!" The elderly woman directed.

The house was full of cats, they were in the hallway and in the lounge.

"Take a seat, just move the cats off the sofa." The Sofa and chairs were blue draylon it matched the curtains and the occupants' recliners.

"Are these all-Persian Cats?" DC Kapoor asked.

"Yes, they are all retired showing and breeding cats." Mrs Swallow said with pride.

"They are absolutely beautiful." DS Carruthers added.

"You had dogs, didn't you?" DC Kapoor asked.

"Yes, I bred Irish setters, but they were getting too big for me. I miss them terribly; I didn't have as many cats then, as I have now." Mrs Swallow laughed.

"I bet they keep you company." DC Kapoor said.

"Yeah, I would be lost without them."

DS Carruthers was feeling a little low since her tom cat 'Pickles' had been dissembled in her kitchen. Seeing the many cats tugged at her heart strings.

Mrs Swallow disappeared and came back with a pot of tea and three homemade blueberry muffins. She placed it on the glass coffee table.

"So, you are here about Sandra de Villiers?"

"Yes." DS Carruthers confirmed.

"It was so sad, to hear that she was murdered."

"How do you know her?" DC Carruthers continued.

"I use to teach her Religious Education at the local grammar school. Then I met her about 10 years ago when she started breeding and showing her Golden retrievers at shows up and down the country. Then when Sandra and Samantha started a ringcraft training group in Grayson I use to go along. Sandra and I became firm friends, she used to come around to help bath and groom my dogs. Twelve months ago, I had to give it up because of my deteriorating health."

"When did you last see Sandra?"

"I saw her on Wednesday 14th December. She brought fish and chips for us both and I baked an apple pie. We had it with Madagascan custard. She used to come around every Tuesday night then at the beginning of November she changed it to a Wednesday."

"Did she give you an explanation why she changed the day?"

"She said she wanted to change the day because she had fallen out with Hugo Molinari at the Dance School and she didn't want Johan to know."

"Do you know why they fell out?"

"Hugo Molinari had been a shoulder to cry on from time to time. He knew about her husbands' womanizing ways. Then Sandra found out about Annabelle. He didn't think she knew, but she knew about everything he got up to. Anyway, she tried ringing me, but I was out at an appointment at Lincoln Hospital in the Orthopaedic out-patients clinic. She left me a message and she sounded upset. Hugo Molinari showered her with affection and they slept together. He was besotted with her, but the feelings were not mutual. All the silly girl wanted was her husband to love her and remain faithful. Hugo Molinari was going through a divorce; his wife ran off with a much younger man. Hugo Molinari was having financial difficulties. He asked Sandra to buy into the Dance School. So, he could pay off his wife, he had already given her the marital home, but that meant he had to sell some of his family's Italian restaurants. But Sandra was not having any of it, her passion was her Golden Retrievers. They had a heated row and she quit her job."

"But why does Johan still think she was at the Dance School on Wednesday and Thursday evenings?"

"Sandra didn't want Johan to know she had quit her job, because he would have wanted to know why? then he would have wanted to speak to Hugo Molinari and Johan would find out about the one-night stand."

"Do you know where she went on Thursday evenings?" DC Kapoor took over the questioning.

"She went to see her brother Daniel. They had just been reunited."

"Do you know when they first met?" DC Kapoor continued.

"I think it was July time this year. They met online then they met at the Coffee House in Stowgarth town centre. Sandra was upset, he lived a very hard life. He didn't have her privileges. Daniel was scrawny, drawn and dishevelled. His clothes were filthy and he had been living on the streets. Sandra could tell he had drug and alcohol problems. She paid for him to stay in a bed & breakfast in Redmile near the river Stow. It was a temporary fix until she sorted something permanent for him. She brought him new clothes and found him a job in a local garden centre. He was doing well. In August she rented a house in New Marsh for him to live in. It was all in her name. She paid the deposit and three months rent up front. Daniel agreed to give her the rent at the beginning of the month. Daniel was cleaning up his act until Richard Downing came on the scene. He moved in with

Daniel to help him cope with the bills. Sandra knew he was trouble with a capital T. Daniel gave up his job and it was a downward spiral. Like I said she went around to see him every Thursday night. Sandra said they all had pizza and watched television. Then she was tragically murdered..."Barbara trailed off.

"Did you know anything about her cocaine abuse?" DS Carruthers interjected.

"I'm sorry, but I did. I tried to tell her, but it went in one ear and out the other. We came to an understanding; she promised not to take it before or when she was with me. I also know that Samantha Mealing had tried to get her to stop too."

They continued talking for about twenty minutes.

"Thank you, you have been very helpful." DS Carruthers said.

"Thank you, the muffins were beautiful." DC Kapoor added.

"Do you think Hugo Molinari is the key to this investigation?" DC Kapoor asked.

"I'm not sure. I think we should go for a coffee. I hate tea, it tastes bloody revolting. Shall we call at the drive through and have an afternoon burger and fries." DS Carruthers sensed they needed a break.

"That sounds good, Serg."

There were only a few cars in the queue. DC Kapoor found a space in the car park they ate their food and drained their cups of coffee. DS Carruthers had rung DC Booth in the incident room and asked to send her Hugo Molinari's previous statement. Moment's later it came through to email box. Both detectives read it. They decided to go and see Hugo Molinari.

When they arrived at the Dance school they were greeted by a very attractive young girl. She was Hugo's niece and she worked on reception. She took them to see Hugo Molinari he was beavering through piles of paperwork.

"How can I help you?" Hugo Molinari tutted and looked at his gold watch.

"I'm sorry if we are disturbing you, but we just have some follow up questions for you regarding the Sandra de Villiers." DS Carruthers began with a sliver of sarcasm.

"We have read your previous statement?" DS Carruthers paused. She showed him, his statement,

"Is this your correct signature?"

"Yeah, that's right, can I ask where this is going. I have loads of work to do." Hugo Molinari said arrogantly.

"If you want, we can do this down the station Mr Molinari?" DS Carruthers said sharply. He looked at her astonished,

"I have done nothing wrong." Hugo Molinari exclaimed.

"You said you had suspended her until she had sorted her cocaine abuse out?"

"That's correct."

"We have a statement that say's that you had an argument because she would not buy into the Dance School. I understand you were having financial difficulties…"

"No that's not the truth. I told you, I suspended her because of her cocaine abuse."

"Did you have a one-night stand with Sandra?" DC Kapoor interjected. Hugo Molinari was lost for words.

"It only happened once, I really liked her and

I thought she liked me? I knew she loved her husband too much to leave him. Sandra was a trophy wife, he showered her in money, it was a loveless marriage. He was too busy screwing all his female employees. All she wanted was to be loved. We could have had so much more." Hugo Molinari said bitterly.

"Was that the only secret you kept?" DC Kapoor asked.

"Do you mean Daniel? That was Sandra's dirty secret. I never divulged it to anyone."

"Anything else you have not told us?"

"NO." Hugo Molinari raised his voice.

"Can I ask why you are so angry?" DS Carruthers asked.

"I was in love with her. I would have done anything for her. I miss her terribly." Hugo Molinari sobbed.

"Thank you, Mr Molinari, we will leave it there." The detectives left the building.

The detectives got back in their unmarked police car. DS Carruthers received a phone call from DI Read that Mr Eccles and his wife had returned home.

"This could be the break we need?" DS Carruthers said with enthusiasm.

They drove off in the direction of Gorton Road.

"It's strange that Hugo Molinari said he suspended Sandra de Villiers because of the cocaine abuse when Daniel Hardy and Mrs Swallow said she left after an argument…" DC Kapoor said.

"Yes, it would be good to find out the truth." DS Carruthers smiled.

"Do you think Hugo Molinari is our blackmailer?" DC Kapoor asked.

"I'm guessing he is, but we need solid proof and at the moment we only have an assumption." DS Carruthers said, she bit her broken fingernail.

"And if it's our blackmailer, is he, our murderer?"

"We should just wait and see. Let's not get a head of ourselves." DS Carruthers said, with a cool head, "We need solid evidence."

"What did you think about the sobbing

outburst?"

"I think it was totally fake, he did it to deflect the truth. He's definitely hiding something."

"Yeah, Serg."

"He might have been in love with Sandra, but she was never going to leave Johan. Hugo Molinari is up to his waist in silage, we will wait until he slips up." DS Carruthers concluded.

The detectives pulled up outside the property on Gorton Road. Purple and black misshapen clouds had appeared in the sky. They looked pregnant with rain. The detectives uneasily peered up at the heavens above. There was an old green estate car on the driveway.

"They must be home." DC Kapoor said.

"No shit sherlock." DS Carruthers laughed.

They got out the car and opened the double gates. They made their way to the front door of the semi-detached house. DS Carruthers knocked loudly on the oak wooden door. A burly bald man in his fifties opened the door. He looked like a bulldog swallowing a wasp. He wore scruffy blue jeans and an oversized blue jumper.

"Are you Mr Eccles?" DS Carruthers asked.

They flashed their police warrants in his direction.

"We arrived home last night. We got your card. I gave the police station a ring this morning."

"Thank you, Mr Eccles, for handing in the missing handbag to the police station. It's a vital piece of evidence. I see you have CCTV. Can we have a look at it. It may help our investigation." DS Carruthers asked.

"Of course, you better come in." The man beckoned them inside.

The house was very warm, but not very inviting. The hallway was dark and full of boxes. The lounge was cluttered and very untidy. It needed decorating the wallpaper and wood work was badly stained with nicotine. A large lady with a ponytail sat on a green sofa with a cigarette in one hand and her oxygen tank in its rubber wheeled carrier beside her. She looked older than her husband. She wore a pink floral dress that was too small for her, rolls of fat bulged for all to see.

"This is my wife, Olive; you can call me Barry." Both detectives said hello.

Mr Eccles moved some boxes and clothes off a very dirty yellow leather sofa. The detectives took a seat. The live CCTV footage appeared on a flatscreen television."

"Can you bring up Friday 16th December 2016 approximately 5pm?" DS Carruthers directed.

"Of course, are you looking for the person that dumped the handbag."

"If we can identify the person, it will help our investigation." DC Kapoor interrupted.

It did not take long to find the correct date and time. They watched the flat screen keenly. At about 17.05 the footage showed someone chucking the handbag into the garden. The person passed the driveway and ran off in the direction of the top end of Gorton Road.

"Can you enlarge the picture, so I can see the person passing your driveway." DS Carruthers asked with anticipation.

"That's our culprit." DC Kapoor said. DS Carruthers could not believe her eyes. They had found Sandra's murderer.

"It looks like it…Mr Eccles can you make a copy of the footage."

Mr Eccles handed her a CD. The detectives thanked him and his wife profusely and disappeared to the car. It was streaming with rain. It was running down the driveway into the gutter onto the road. The detectives got wet through, but they did not care, they had found their murderer.

DS Carruthers and DC Kapoor put the CD on her laptop and showed DCI Barnes and DI Read the footage from Gorton Road. She enlarged the picture.

"It's Hugo Molinari." DS Carruthers told him about the talk they had with him earlier.

"We have got him, well done guys…The cold-hearted bastard. He sent her a text while she was in church hall and lured her outside to her death." DCI Barnes did not spare the rod.

"Well, that seems that way, guv." DS Carruthers replied.

"Shall we bring him in?" DC Kapoor said excitedly.

"Certainly, arrest him, bring him in now…You and DC Kapoor can go and arrest him and then call SOCO I want the warehouse apartments ripped to bits."

CHAPTER TWENTY-NINE
Friday 30th December 2016

The briefing didn't take long that morning. DS Munro and her team had been called away to a suspicious death in a warden aided complex in Sandwell.

"You will be pissed off like me that they didn't find anything to link Hugo Molinari at dance school or his third-floor apartment. We do have his car a blue people carrier. It was seen outside Sylvia Harris' house on the evening of the murder. Hugo Molinari' vehicle was taken away and is with forensics. We are just waiting for the results. It's important that we get these results as our other findings at the moment are a bit flimsy and Hugo Molinari' brief is Mr Raab. And his professionalism and cunning precedes him. Once we can charge him, we can build a solid case for the CPS. We will interview him and hopefully charge him this afternoon…You have got plenty of work to get on with. So, I will speak to you again soon." DCI Barnes strolled purposely into his office, DI Read followed him like a lost lamb.

DS Carruthers team was back to full strength, she briefed DC Dempster and DC Dimka with what happened yesterday at Mrs Swallows and at Barry Eccles. Then they all ploughed through the internal and external emails.

DC Kapoor brought DS Carruthers a double expresso from the hot drinks machine.

"This report as come from uniformed. Hugo's cousin would like to help us with our enquiries. She is presently looking after the twin boys until their mother comes back from holiday. I have the address."

"Thank you, the more evidence we can get on him, the stronger the case." DS Carruthers stated.

Hugo Molinari, cousin Miss Molinari lived in apartment in Sandwell. It was clean, spacious and very modern in taste. She answered the intercom straight away and let them into the building. Miss Molinari opened the door, she was tall, slim and very attractive.

I'm DS Carruthers and this is DC Kapoor. We have come about your cousin Hugo Molinari." The detectives showed their police warrants.

Miss Molinari welcomed them into the apartment. They all sat around the solid wooden kitchen table. The twin boys were with her partner Miss Plummer.

"What do you do for a profession?" DS

Carruthers began.

"I'm a chartered accountant, it's my own business. That's how I manage to be able to teach dance and I look after the twins once or twice a week."

"How can you help us?" DC Kapoor interrupted. He was a bit over zealous. DS Carruthers just glared at him.

"I was there when you arrested my cousin for the murder of Sandra de Villiers. When I took the twins home, I looked up the date of the murder on my browser then I read the report that they wanted any witnesses who was in the vicinity at around 5pm. Then it dawned on me. Friday 16th December 2016 was the day after my birthday. I had a dance lesson and I was about to leave for home when Hugo rang me from his apartment. He said he had an urgent call from Bellisimo his Italian restaurant in Stowgarth town centre. The new computerized POS had gone on the blink again. He asked if I could look after the boys, so I locked up and went upstairs to his apartment.

"What time was this?" DS Carruthers probed.
"It was just before 4pm? I told him he had to be back for 6.30pm because I teach ballroom and Latin to adults with special needs."

"How did he get to the restaurant?"

"He drove there, your colleagues took his car away to the police station."

"Can I ask what time Hugo left and returned home?" DS Carruthers probed further.

"He went out around 4.10pm he had ordered a pizza for us all, and he come home around 5.40pm."

"How was he when he came back?"

"To be honest a bit strange, he rushed straight in and went for a shower. When he came out, I went down to open up for my dance students…I thought something was strange the following day. I was just arriving to open up for a dance class. Hugo was valeting his car in the heavy snow. Unlike him. He normally has it done at the car wash in town, the one facing the train station.

"Is Hugo going to be charged with Sandra de Villiers murder?"

"We can't say at this time, but you will know in due course.

"Hugo said he was in love with her? Why would he do something like that?"

"What did you think of Sandra de Villiers?" DC Kapoor interrupted.

"She was a fantastic dancer and teacher, but we never really got on."

"Why was that?"

"She didn't like my choice of sexuality and having a daughter…You met here yesterday. She was the girl on reception in the dance school. I think she was jealous because she could not conceive."

"Thank you. DC Kapoor will take a statement from you. You have been very informative."

Hugo Molinari and his solicitor Mr Raab sat facing DCI Barnes and DS Carruthers. DI Read and DC Kapoor watched and listened from the observation room.

DS Carruthers pressed the record button on the digital recorder. Everyone around the table introduced themselves. DS Carruthers began with some basic questions then DCI Barnes started questioning Hugo Molinari.

"You said in your last statement that you had a one-night stand with Sandra de Villiers. Was you hurt when she would not leave her husband for you." DCI Barnes straight to the nitty gritty.

"You mean I couldn't give her the security that she had from her husband. He showered her with money and he cheated on her many times." Hugo Molinari replied.

"Were you blackmailing Sandra de Villiers?"

"No, definitely not, I loved her!"

"Remember! Mr Molinari what I said before the interview." Mr Raab insisted. He touched his client's arm.

"You said you suspended Sandra de Villiers because of her cocaine abuse or was that another lie?" DS Carruthers interrupted bluntly.

"No comment." Hugo Molinari looked at his solicitor and smiled.

DS Carruthers thought *"If he's telling the truth, that means Sandra said they had fallen out because she didn't want them to know she had been suspended. It was probably one of those things that we will never know the truth."*

"Did you murder Sandra de Villiers?" DCI Barnes asked.

"No comment!" Hugo Molinari insisted.

"Two eyewitnesses saw you at about 4.55pm going in the direction of Church Street. Your photo and eight other men who look like you were shown to the eyewitnesses and you were identified by them both. You said you was at home with your boys at the time of the murder. We have a statement from your cousin that she looked after the boys because you had urgently been called into your restaurant in Stowgarth. You left just after 4pm and arrived back at 5.40pm."

DS Carruthers showed him the CCTV footage from 22 Gorton Road. It showed a person throwing something into the garden, but when the person passed the driveway. It was clear it was Hugo Molinari.

DS Carruthers thought *We have thrown the kitchen sink at him, without positive forensics from the car, do we have enough evidence to charge him. The other option could be to hold him an extra twelve hours, but we need the police commissioner's permission.*

There was a knock on the door to the interview room,

"Come in!" DCI Barnes shouted.

"Can I have a word please?" It was DI Read.

"Excuse me guys, we will only be a moment." DCI Barnes apologised. The detectives opened the door and went out into the corridor, shutting the door firmly behind them.

"I hope it's good news, you know I don't like any interruptions when I'm interviewing, especially when someone is getting questioned regarding a murder." DCI Barnes seethed.

"Sorry, Guv." A red-faced DI Read apologised, "There were traces of Sandra's blood found in Hugo Molinari' car, in the footwell and on the driver's pedals. More than likely transferred there from his size nine boots. It looks like he tried to clean the driver's side of the car, but he didn't clean all of it."

"That's fantastic news…" The detectives were all overjoyed. They had found the evidence that would send him down.

"Also, uniformed need to interview him in regards to arranging the beating of Cody Scott, we have solid proof, we have the transaction of cash on mobile footage and we have the lad who beat him to a pulp. So, once he has been officially charged can they talk to him." DI Read asked.

"Of course."

The DCI and DS Carruthers went back in the interview room.

The detectives went back to their seats, the digital recorder was un-paused.

"Well, Well, Mr Molinari." DCI Barnes had his elbows on the table and the palms of his hands arched.

"Did-you-murder-Sandra-de-Villiers?"

"NO COMMENT!" Hugo Molinari said an octave higher.

"Are you still playing that game?" DS Carruthers interrupted. Hugo Molinari smiled like a Cheshire cat.

"We have forensic results from your car and you tried your best to clean up the blood in the footwell and on the pedals. People think by cleaning it gets rid of the blood, but there is always some left behind…Hugo Molinari I am charging you with the murder of Sandra de Villiers." The DCI announced. Hugo Molinari lowered his gaze. All his bravado had been extinguished.

"My twin son's what's going to happen to them." Hugo sobbed like a baby.

DS Carruthers took him to the custody desk. He was officially charged then he was taken to another interview room.

The Incident room was cacophony of noise. Inside the last few days, they had solved two cases. Everyone was jubilant. DCS Hargreaves came down to the department and thanked everyone. At the end of the shift, they all went over to the Stag Inn.

CHAPTER THIRTY

The Stag Inn was kind of busy this evening, all the detectives from the Serious Crime Unit were present even DCS Hargreaves had turned-up. He had been drinking with top brass as he had officially retired today. He proudly brought everyone a drink. DCI Barnes, DCS Hargreaves and DS Carruthers stood at the bar while DS Munro collecting her free drink. She heard the senior detectives showering DS Carruthers with praise. DS Munro saw her walk towards the female toilet. DS Munro was standing at the sink area when DS Carruthers came out the toilet cubicle. DS Munro was a boiling pan of milk ready to boil over.

"Don't you think both our teams should get the credit, not just you." DS Munro said angrily.

"Sorry I don't know what you mean?" DS Carruthers asked.

"I heard you getting all the praise from DCI Barnes and that poisonous toad DCS Hargreaves."

"Look Kate, I always praise my team. It's up to you to praise yours!" DS Carruthers snapped. She washed her hands and walked out of the toilets with a wry smile on her face.

DS Carruthers made her way to the bar, there was no DC Kapoor. DC Dempster tapped her on her shoulder,

"You looking for DC Kapoor?"

"Yeah." DS Carruthers smiled.

"He has just gone outside to take a call."
"Oh, ok?"

"What are drinking Serg?" DC Dempster asked.

"I have a pint of lager and DC Kapoor will have a fresh orange and lemonade."

When they arrived at the Stag Inn it was sort of light, but now it was dark outside. The rain finally stopped, the air smelled fresh and a fog had descended upon the town. They made their way back to the police station. The staff car park was virtually empty except for Vikram's brand-new lease car. It was a German make and a sports edition. It had been delivered to him earlier that morning by the dealership. They got in the vehicle. Vikram had to put his seat right back because of his long legs.

"Oh, it looks and feels fantastic." Faith ran her hand up and down the leather upholstery.

"It should be, for what I'm paying every month." Vikram snapped.

"You did not have to get a lease car because I suggested it, I just thought you don't have to pay for repairs, tax and insurance is included and every year you get a new car. It's a win-win situation."

Vikram agreed and apologised for being short.

"What's been wrong with you? These last few days? You have been short and unprofessional at times. It's unlike you?" Faith asked with concern.
"Just family stuff, my parents are not happy with my decision not to marry Chadda."

"OK, that makes sense, sorry."

They drove in the direction of Faith's home. In the last few week's, it had become his second home too. Vikram was pleased with his new car's effortless punch through the streets. It had to be careful because of the dense fog.

"There must have been a power cut." Faith announced.

"No, your lamp is still on and your blind is closed…Did we leave it switched on this morning when we left for work?"

"We must have done." Faith shrugged her shoulders.

Vikram parked his new car outside Faith's house. Faith opened the door and walked into the hallway; something did not feel right. Vikram was dawdling behind her somewhere. Instead of going into the kitchen she turned right into the lounge.

"Hello Faith." Her heart sank lower than the deepest ocean.

"Ronnie!" Faith exclaimed. She put her hand to her mouth in shock. Her step daughter was sitting in Faith's chair with a gun in her hand.

"Ronnie looked like her dad. She was 5foot9, round, sleeve tattoo's, piercing blue eyes and long black hair.

"Faith." Vikram shouted.

Ronnie leaped from her seat and yanked Faith towards her. She wrapped her arms around her, holding her very tight. She pointed the gun at her head.

Vikram entered the lounge he had taken off his black turban. He had shorted shaved hair.

"Hiya Vik."

"You know him? She struggled to say. Ronnie turned Faith around and threw her on the chair and pointed the gun at her.

"How do you know Vikram?" Faith asked inaudibly.

"I found out that you had been transferred here to Stowgarth, then I put a plan in action. I seduced Vikram at the Stag Inn and he was putty in my hands. Then we kind of fell in love. He did, I didn't he was just a means to an end." Ronnie smiled at Vikram.

"So, it's been a set-up?" Faith said. She thought *"Was this whole relationship a sham. Did Vikram have no feelings for me at all. It was just a game to get close to me."*

"Yes, from start to finish. I broke into your house; I torched Vik's car then I killed your pussy cat. While Vik wined and dined you." Ronnie replied. Faith tried to get up, but Ronnie threw her back in the chair.

"How come you enlisted Vikram's help?"

"It did not make much working out, once I had inside information."

"DC Windass." DS Carruthers said.

"Yes, he gave me the information for a price…Who you were working with? Then like I said he was putty in my hands." Ronnie laughed.

Vikram did not even flinch with what was said. DS Carruthers hated to think it, but he was up to his eye's balls in it.

"Why? Ronnie Why?" I have always been good to you."

"My dad is on remand because of you, he may go to prison and you know what the inmates will do to him once they know he was a copper. If I shoot you then there will be no case. No shining VICTIM." Ronnie said. The hatred in the room was palpable.

"Why did you inform your colleagues in CID about my dad?"

"Look, me and your dad finished when he tried to kill me. I was his puppet on his string. I did whatever he told me to do. In or out of work he monitored who I saw, what I wore and where I went. He stopped me from seeing my family and friends. He didn't like me going out after work. He even tracked my phone. There were threats to my life, if I did not behave. Your dad controlled me and when I wouldn't have sex with him, he raped and physically beat me. He never touched my face, but used me as a punchbag. He chipped away at my self-esteem. I was no longer outlandish and confident. Your dad ruined my life and when I finally had the courage to stand up to him, he didn't like it." Faith was nearly in tears.

"You're a liar, my dad loved you, he cherished you, I saw it?" Ronnie shouted.

"You saw what we wanted you to see?"

Ronnie pointed the gun to Faith's head.

"Vik, I advise you to go before I have to shoot you as well."

"I'm not going anywhere!" Vikram stood still.

Ronnie turned the gun on Faith again. Faith sobbed; she knew that she was as dangerous as her dad. She had been sacked by the Cornwall and Devon Police for buying, selling and the distribution of drugs and laundering money. She did her sentence in Stopsley women's HM Prison.

Ronnie moved forward with gun pointed at Faith. She was about to shoot at her. When Faith reached and picked up the empty crystal decanter of the table by her chair. In one full swoop she smashed it over Ronnies head. As she fell to the floor, she squeezed the trigger and the bang echoed around Ivy Street.

"No." Faith shouted. Vikram had been shot; he lay in a pool of blood. Ronnie was out for the count, blood pouring from her head. Faith phoned for an ambulance and the police were dispatched. Faith tried to stem the bleeding from Vikram's chest, but she could see she was fighting a losing battle. He was in and out of consciousness.

"Faith." Vikram whispered. He struggled to get his words out.

"Hush, don't speak, save your energy, everything is going to be alright."

"I'm sorry, I do love you."

"I love you." Faith kissed his cheek. She thought *"I know Ronnie was behind all this. Vikram was just collateral damage. She used him to get to me."*

Vikram closed his eyes and then he was gone. *"NO, NO, NO, NO."* Faith screamed.

"The paramedics arrived at the crime scene, but Vikram was already dead. The police arrived and were told what happened and who shot Vikram.

Ronnie was conscious, but dazed.

"YOU BITCH, I WILL GET YOU FOR THIS!!!." Ronnie sniped.

PC Sanders went with Ronnie to the hospital while DC Dimka sat in his car with Faith while waiting for SOCO to arrive.

Faith thought *"I have found the armed robbers, and Sandra de Villiers murderer, but I could not see that Vikram was playing me. Why couldn't Ronnie believe that her dad was a complete control freak and he made my life hell. Vikram is dead, but the romance felt real, what am I supposed to believe. He said he loved me, but did he? I suppose I can just hold on to the times we had together. I'm hurt and devastated, will I ever find the right man. I seem to attract the bad ones. Let's just hope I get the new DI position if I don't, I will move on."*

Printed in Great Britain
by Amazon